Bad Boy

He had his back to me, but I knew right away who it was. No mistake. No *possible* mistake. The guy that Judy MacWilliams was heading into the movies with was James Baker.

Amanda's boyfriend! With Judy MacWilliams! Together! The two of them!

And Judy turned her head and looked straight at me and shot me a great big, triumphant smile. And I knew exactly what that smile meant.

'Next time you see Amanda,' Judy's smile meant, 'don't forget to tell her that you saw the two of us together!'

Little Sister books published by Red Fox

Book 1: The Great Sister War
Book 2: My Sister, My Slave
Book 3: Stacy the Matchmaker
Book 4: Copycat
Book 5: Sneaking Out
Book 6: Sister Switch
Book 7: Full House
Book 8: Bad Boy

Bad Boy

ALLAN FREWIN JONES

Series created by
Ben M. Baglio

RED FOX

A Red Fox Book

Published by Random House Children's Books
20 Vauxhall Bridge Road, London SW1V 2SA

A division of Random House UK Ltd
London Melbourne Sydney Auckland
Johannesburg and agencies throughout the world

1 3 5 7 9 10 8 6 4 2

First published in Great Britain by Red Fox 1996

Set in 12 on 14pt Plantin
Phototypeset by Intype London Ltd
Printed and bound in Great Britain by
Cox & Wyman Ltd, Reading, Berkshire

RANDOM HOUSE UK Limited Reg. No. 954009

ISBN 0 09 966641 3

Chapter One

My big sister Amanda has finally gotten herself a boyfriend. Amanda is thirteen, and when a girl hits thirteen, it's really important for her to have a boyfriend. At least, that's what Amanda says.

I wouldn't know about that myself. I'm ten, which means that I've got more interesting things to do with my time than go out with boys. My name's Stacy Allen, by the way, and I live in Four Corners, Indiana, with my mom and dad, my baby brother Sam, my cat, Benjamin, and my crazy big sister, Amanda.

Amanda's new boyfriend is called James Baker.

A recent entry in Stacy Allen's Private, Confidential and Top Secret Diary

I like James. If I wanted to go out with a boy, I'd choose someone just like James. He's nice looking and really smart. I don't know WHAT he sees in Amanda!

To be honest, that last bit isn't completely true. I *do* know what he *sees* in her. I mean, my sister Amanda isn't exactly ugly. In fact, she's kind of good looking if you like the empty-headed, curly blonde-haired, long-legged, big-smiling, all-American cheerleader type.

Any boy who wanted to date *me*, on the other hand, would have to like the flat-brown-haired, skinny-ribbed, twig-legged, freckle-faced, teeth-braced, homely-but-really-interesting type.

It is kind of strange that Amanda and I look so *different*. It's like, before we were born, Amanda lined up *twice* in the good looks department but forgot to go to the *brains* department, if you know what I mean.

Amanda and James had been dating for about three weeks when the stuff that I'm going to tell you about happened. And in that three weeks – in twenty one whole days – Amanda and I hadn't had a single argument. Well, not unless you count me getting mad at her because she was spending forever in the bathroom *preening* herself when I needed to get in there pretty urgently.

In fact, Amanda had been in such a good

mood ever since she'd started dating James, that she'd even lent me her portable CD player, which was pretty much a miracle. She usually threatened to kill me if I even *looked* at it.

So you can see why the Amanda and James set-up was good news in the Allen household.

But I had one worry.

James is really smart. I don't mean he's some kind of nerd, but he does have a *brain*. The thing that was worrying me was that it wouldn't take anyone with a brain more than ten minutes to realize that my big sister Amanda is something of an airhead.

Amanda's got her good points. Like, she's the best artist in the whole school. You should see some of the paintings and drawings she's done. They're totally amazing.

But after three weeks I figured that Amanda would have said all there was to say about art. And what else did Amanda know about? Well, she could talk for *hours* about Eddie Eden, her all-time favourite pop singer. She could talk for *ever* about hairstyles and trendy clothes and nail polish and mind-blowingly boring stuff like that. The sort of dumb stuff that Amanda and her brain-dead Bimbo friends were *always* talking about.

The trouble was, how long would it take for James to get utterly sick and tired of hearing about Eddie Eden and hairdos and clothes?

I put this question to my friends, Pippa, Cindy and Fern in the school cafeteria one lunchtime.

'Maybe James doesn't think Amanda is boring at all,' Cindy said.

'Get real,' I said. 'He must!'

'Don't be so sure,' Pippa said. 'How many dates have they been on?'

'I don't know,' I said. 'I haven't been keeping score.'

'Approximately,' Pippa said. Pippa likes long words. Her mom is a college professor, so I guess that's where she gets it from. I like long words too. Words like *hamburger* and *chocolatemilkshake* and *pepperonipizzawithextra-cheese*.

'Approximately lots,' I said.

'There you go,' Pippa said.

'There I go, *where*?' I asked.

'There you go where Cindy said,' Pippa said.

'What did I say?' Cindy asked, looking up from her yoghurt container where she'd been busy fishing out the strawberry chunks with her spoon. 'I didn't say anything.'

'Yes, you did,' Pippa said. 'You said maybe James doesn't think Amanda is boring. Would

8

he have been on lots of dates with her if he thought she was boring? Of course not!'

I still wasn't convinced.

'Maybe he just hasn't *realized* it yet,' I said. 'Maybe one day he'll wake up and say, "Hey, Amanda never talks about anything interesting. I've had enough of *her*!" '

'So, what if he did?' Fern asked suspiciously. 'Why are you so interested in who Amanda goes out with?'

'Because James is really nice,' I said. 'If Amanda's going to have a boyfriend, I'd rather it was someone like James than some total dork like Tony Scarfoni or Matt Taylor.' Tony and Matt were a couple of good-looking deadheads from the eighth grade. The kind of boys I'd expect Amanda to want to go out with.

'If you ask me, I think Stacy likes James herself,' Fern said with a big grin.

'No one asked you!' I snapped. 'And I don't like James – not like *that*, anyway. I just like him as a person. Can't a person even *like* another person without certain people trying to make a big deal out of it?'

'Calm down, Stacy,' Fern said. 'I was only kidding.'

'Yeah, *well*,' I said grouchily, 'the fact is that life with Amanda has been a whole lot easier since she got a regular boyfriend.' I frowned at Fern. 'Whoever he happens to be. And I don't want her regular boyfriend to stop dating her, because Amanda will get upset if that happens. And when Amanda gets upset she's a total and utter pain in the neck.'

I took a deep breath. 'So,' I continued, 'we need to come up with some ideas for how I can make sure James keeps going out with my sister for as long as possible. Some cunning and sneaky ways to keep them together even after James has realized what an airhead my sister really is.'

'The way I see it,' Pippa said, 'I think you should keep right out of it.' She gave me one of her superior my-mom's-a-professor looks. 'Any intervention by you is just bound to be catastrophic!'

The rest of us just looked at her.

'Catty-what?' Fern asked.

'Strophic,' Pippa said. 'It means really, really bad.'

'So why didn't you say so?' Cindy asked.

'I did.'

'No, you didn't.' Fern said. 'You said catty-stroppy-something.'

'Can I help it if I've got a bigger vocabulary than the rest of you?' Pippa said.

'Huh!' Fern grunted. 'At least people know what I mean when I open my mouth.'

'Let's not argue,' I said, giving Pippa a

quick hug. 'Thanks, Pippa. You said just what I hoped you'd say.'

Pippa just blinked at me.

I guess I should explain. Pippa Kane is definitely one of my very best friends. But there's one thing about Pippa that everyone needs to know: if she ever gives advice, or says that she's got a really good idea, you should *always* do the exact opposite of what she says. Pippa's advice is always terrible, and Pippa's good ideas always end up as total disasters. Catty-stroppies, even.

So, when Pippa told me I shouldn't mess around with James and Amanda, I just *knew* that I should get involved as soon as possible.

As soon as possible turned out to be that evening.

I was up in my room giving Benjamin a thorough combing. He was shedding, so I had to comb out all the loose hair at least once a day. It would have been ten times a day if Benjamin had his way!

We were sitting on my bed. At least, I was sitting. Benjamin likes to prowl around while he's being combed, so I was doing my best to get rid of all the excess fur while he walked up and down and around and around, *murrping* and *prurrping* and trying to bite the handle off the comb.

I was just about through with Benjamin

when I heard the front door open. I heard Amanda say, 'Come on in,' to someone.

And then she yelled, 'Mom! I'm home. James and me are going to watch a video.'

That was my cue for action.

Operation Keep James Entertained was about to take off.

The way I saw it, if James started to get bored by Amanda, it was up to *me*, her interesting and extremely intelligent younger sister, to entertain him.

I grabbed a video I'd borrowed from the school library and raced downstairs.

'Hi, Amanda, hi, James,' I said. 'Who wants to watch *this*?' I held up the video.

Amanda squinted at it. '*Arctic Adventure*?' she read. ' "A year in the life of a *polar bear*"?' She looked at me. 'Are you kidding me, or what?'

'It's really good,' I said. 'It's about this mother polar bear and her two cubs.' I looked at James. 'And there's this part right at the end where a leopard seal is looking for a meal, and one of the baby polar bears is getting closer and closer to where this leopard seal is lying in wait, and – '

'Stacy!' Amanda interrupted. 'We don't want to watch some dumb *animal* movie.'

'James might,' I said. I gave James a big

smile. 'You'd like to see it, wouldn't you, James?'

James shrugged. 'Why not?'

'Because I've borrowed *this* from Cheryl,' Amanda said, waving a videotape under my nose. 'And I said I would give it back to her tomorrow, so if we don't watch it now, we won't get a chance to watch it at all.'

I grabbed hold of the video so I could read the title.

'*Cheerleader Champions Take On the World?*' I read with a groan. 'James doesn't want to watch *that!*'

'Yes he does,' Amanda said. She looked at James. 'Don't you?'

James smiled at me. 'Maybe we could watch your video some other time, Stacy.'

'Yeah,' Amanda mumbled as she towed James into the living room. 'And maybe we *couldn't.*'

'It's really interesting,' I said. 'Honest, it is.'

Amanda looked around at me. 'Does the leopard seal get to eat the little polar bear?'

'No, of course not,' I said. 'The momma bear comes along and rescues it.'

'Aw, heck,' Amanda said. 'Now you've gone and told us how it ends, Stacy. Oh, well, I guess there's no point in us watching it now!'

So much for part one of *Operation Keep*

James Entertained. Amanda had put a stop to that pretty quickly.

But I couldn't leave James to suffer through a whole *Cheerleader Champions* video. The poor guy would just die of boredom.

I had to think of something else. And I had to think quickly. If I watched the movie with them, then I could keep James entertained while Amanda was glued to the screen. It was worth a try.

'Can I watch *Cheerleader Champions* with you?' I asked.

Amanda frowned at me. 'Just so long as you keep quiet.'

'I smiled at her. 'Sure, I will,' I said.

Chapter Two

'This is the stupidest film I've ever seen in my entire life,' I said.

'So why don't you go and do something else?' Amanda said.

'Nah,' I said. 'It's OK. I can put up with it if James can.'

Amanda, James and I were sitting on the couch in the living room, watching *Cheerleader Champions Take On the World*.

Boy, was it a stupid movie! The head cheerleader, a dumb blonde girl called Kimberly, had been kidnapped only two days before the squad was meant to be performing at the International Cheerleading Competition. And by some total miracle, her sidekick, Emma, had figured that they'd taken her to a lonely cabin in some woods just over the Canadian border.

'I mean, come *on*!' I said. 'How the heck did Emma figure *that* out?'

'Because Kimberly's cousin, Ralph, heard Mrs Duchovski from the gas station say that

15

she heard Boris talking to Vladimir about making sure they had enough fuel to get them to Morgan County,' James explained. 'And Coach Freemantle had that list of vacation cabins that Freddie found, and there was only that *one* cabin in Morgan County, so they figured that Boris must have taken Kimberly there.' James smiled at me. 'See?'

'Well, *yeah*, I guess so,' I said. 'But I thought Flick Armstrong came in and interrupted Freddie before he had time to get a good look at the list.'

'No,' James said. 'That wasn't Freddie. That was the guy from the convenience store who was trying to dig up some dirt on Principal Edwards and that woman in the green dress.'

'Oh, yeah! Right! I remember!' I said. 'But I thought he took the list away. So how come Freddie found it?'

'Will you two *shut up*!' Amanda hollered. 'I can't hear a word they're saying!' She jabbed her thumb down on the rewind button of the remote control. 'I'm going to have to watch that scene over again now.'

'I don't know why you're bothering,' I said. 'I can tell you how it'll end right now. They'll rescue Kimberly and her squad will win the competition.'

Amanda pushed the stop button. 'I'm going

16

to get a Coke. James, would you like something to drink?'

'Coke would be fine,' James said.

Amanda headed for the door.

'I'd like a Coke, too,' I called after her.

'Well, why don't you get yourself one, Stacy?' Amanda shouted from the hall. 'They've got them stacked sky high down at the supermarket.'

Well, ha, ha, Amanda!

I smiled at James. 'Are you interested in wildlife at all?' I asked. 'I get a monthly wildlife magazine sent to me. I could lend you some of them.'

'Yeah, I'd like that,' James said.

'Mom wants you, Stacy,' Amanda said as she came back in with two cans of Coke.

'What for?' I asked.

'How should I know?' Amanda said. 'She called up from the basement. You'd better go and see.'

I got up. 'I didn't hear her,' I said.

'She sounded like it was pretty urgent, Stacy,' she said.

I ran down the basement stairs. My mom's got an office down there. My parents converted it a few years ago so Mom could work from home.

Mom is a proofreader. She checks books for spelling and good grammar before they

17

get properly printed. She mostly works on these really dull academic books, but she takes a break every now and then by writing rhymes for greetings cards.

Mom was tapping away at her keyboard. She had her headphones on, which meant she was probably listening to some of that old-fashioned rock music that she and Dad like.

She didn't look around, so I guessed she hadn't heard me.

I tapped her on the shoulder and she nearly shot straight up through the ceiling.

'Stacy!' she gasped, pulling her headphones off. 'Don't *do* that!'

'Sorry,' I said. 'What did you want?'

She looked at me. 'What do you mean, what do *I* want?' she asked. 'You came down here.'

'Amanda said you wanted me.'

Mom shook her head. 'Not me, honey,' she said.

It took me about three seconds to figure out what was going on.

Amanda had set this up to get rid of me.

I ran back upstairs. At first I was just going to walk straight back in there, but then I saw that they were sitting really close together, and James was smiling at Amanda like he was really enjoying himself.

18

I figured maybe Amanda didn't need my help right then to keep James entertained.

* * *

I kept out of their way for the rest of the evening.

I mean, I can take a *hint*.

Later on, I was sitting in the kitchen, dangling a piece of ribbon while Benjamin jumped and clawed at it, when I heard Amanda and James in the hall. It sounded like James was about to go home.

'Will you miss me while I'm away?' I heard Amanda ask James. She and the rest of the cheerleading squad were going to cheerleading camp for the weekend.

'Of course I will,' James said. 'What time are you back?'

'Not until late Sunday afternoon,' Amanda said. 'So you've got to do without me for two whole days. Are you going to be doing anything?'

'I think I'm going to the movies on Saturday,' James said. 'Judy MacWilliams told me they're showing *Speedfreaks* in the afternoon. A sneak preview.'

'As long as you're not going *with* Judy MacWilliams,' Amanda said. 'I don't want you going anywhere *near* her.'

Judy MacWilliams is Amanda's arch-rival

at school. I mean, they totally *hate* each other. In fact, Judy quit the cheerleading squad just because Amanda got the job of squad leader. (Amanda would probably have done the same if Judy had been picked. Things are *that* bad between them.)

'Judy seems OK to me,' James said.

'Take my word for it,' Amanda said. 'She isn't OK at all. She's a total rat-toad-skunk-creep-monster-from-the-black-swamp-*thing*!'

'You don't like her much, do you?' James said.

'I don't even want to discuss her,' Amanda said. 'As far as I'm concerned, Judy MacWilliams doesn't even exist!'

I heard the front door open. They chatted for a while longer out front, and then I heard Amanda come back into the house.

I went into the hall.

'I bet James was bored out of his mind by that movie,' I said.

Amanda tossed her hair as she walked upstairs. 'For your information,' she said, 'he totally enjoyed it.'

'He *did*?' I said, following her up the stairs. 'But it was such a dumb story. I bet they rescued Kimberly and I bet the squad won the championships.'

'Of course they did,' Amanda said. She turned and looked at me. 'James enjoyed it because he was with *me*. He told me he'd enjoy doing *anything* so long as it was with me.' She patted me on the head. (Grrr! I hate that!) 'You just don't understand, Stacy.'

She walked into her room and closed the door.

Well, she was right about that. I *didn't* understand.

But if James *really* liked Amanda, then that was just fine with me. And if he didn't mind her being an airhead, that was even better.

Chapter Three

I was woken up really early the next morning when Amanda came crashing into my room. She grabbed her CD player off my beside table and stomped back out.

'Hey,' I called. 'What's the big idea?'

'I need it for camp,' she called. 'I'm really sorry I woke you.' Yeah, I bet she was!

I sat up and rubbed my eyes. On normal Saturday mornings Amanda didn't appear until nearly lunch time. But this Saturday morning my dad was taking her to cheerleading camp. And if Amanda was up early, then she was going to make darned sure everyone else was up early, too.

Benjamin sat up and yawned. Up until about a month ago, Benjamin had always slept on my bed. But now his favourite bed was in the lap of a gigantic blue and white stuffed rabbit which sits in the corner of my room. The rabbit is as tall as I am, and he's got these huge feet that stick up about a yard in the air, and these great long, floppy ears. He really belongs to my Aunt Susie, but I'm looking after him. It'd take too long to explain *why* I'm looking after him. He's called Donovan.

Benjamin came and jumped on my stomach. That's a sure sign that he needs feeding.

I got dressed and we wandered downstairs to the kitchen.

The kitchen was full of Bimbos. Cheryl Ruddick was there, and so was Rachel Goldstein and Natalie Smith, Amanda's best friends. I think of them as the Hyena, the Gibbon and the Gopher. I guess that's unfair on real hyenas, gibbons and gophers, but it is kind of what the three of them look like.

'Hi, it's Benjie-wenjie,' Cheryl Hyena said as we went into the kitchen. 'Who's a cutesie-wootsie, then?' And she bent over and picked Benjamin up. She's always doing that, and Benjamin really hates being picked up by strange people.

Note that Cheryl said *hi* to Benjamin but ignored me. That's typical Bimbo behaviour.

'He'll scratch you if you don't put him down,' I warned Cheryl as I headed over to the cabinet to get a can of cat food.

'You won't scratch me, will you, Benjie-wenjie?' Cheryl simpered. 'That silly girl doesn't know what good friends we are. *Ow!*'

Benjamin had had enough of *that*! He

squirmed out of Cheryl's arms and dug a couple of claws into her as he made his jump for freedom.

'Told you so,' I said.

The kitchen floor was covered in bags and cases. From all the luggage, anyone would think that this cheerleading camp was going to last a month.

'Dumb cat!' Cheryl moaned, rubbing her arm.

'Yeah,' Rachel said. 'Kind of like its owner.' They all had a little snigger at this.

I opened the tin and forked some food into Benjamin's bowl. 'You should be careful you don't catch *fleas*,' I said.

All three of them made a flying leap away from Benjamin.

'Ew! Does he have fleas?' Natalie whined. 'That's so gross!'

'I was talking to *Benjamin*,' I said with a big cheesy grin. 'I don't want him catching things off *you*.'

Mom came in, carrying Sam.

'Hi, girls,' she said. 'Looking forward to camp?'

'We sure are,' Cheryl said. 'Is Amanda ready yet?'

'Ready as I'll ever be.' Amanda puffed as she dragged a suitcase into the kitchen. 'I hope I've thought of everything.'

I went and sat on the stairs to call Cindy on the phone. I was still waiting for someone to pick up at the other end when Dad came past me down the stairs.

'Hey! Guys!' he called. 'Time to go!'

There was a couple of minutes of chaos as the Bimbo Brigade dragged their thirty million bags out to the car. They were all shouting and yelling at once and sounding like a stampeding herd of elephants.

Mom waved them goodbye and closed the door. She wiped her hand across her forehead and grinned at me.

'Phew!' she said. 'Peace!' And then Sam let out this yell from the kitchen and Mom had to go and see what the problem was.

I put the phone down. No one had answered. I thought that was kind of strange, because we always call each other on Saturday morning to decide what we were going to do for the weekend.

I called Fern. She told me she'd called Cindy last night and there hadn't been an answer then, either. But neither of us could figure out what was going on with Cindy.

'Maybe they've all gone out shopping?' Fern said.

'That doesn't explain no one answering the phone last night,' I said.

'Oh, well,' Fern said. 'It beats me. Hey, did

you know *Mayhem at Mindy's* is showing in town?'

Mayhem at Mindy's was a movie that had just been released. I'd seen a review of it on television, and it had gotten five stars and four smiley faces, which means it's a one hundred percent brilliant film and very nearly one hundred percent totally funny. It was about a bunch of teenage girls who try to arrange a big party at their school. And from what the reviewer had said, *everything* goes wrong.

'They're showing it this afternoon,' Fern said. 'Why don't we go? I'll call Pippa. You keep trying Cindy.'

I checked with Mom that it was OK for me to go then ran back to the phone to arrange when and where we'd all meet up.

'One o'clock at the fountain in the mall,' Fern said. 'And keep trying Cindy!'

I must have called Cindy's number about a hundred times that morning and *no one* answered. If they were out shopping, it had to be the longest shopping trip *ever*.

In the end I had to set off for the mall without getting in touch with Cindy.

Pippa was already sitting on one of the stone benches around the fountain. The fountain is right in the middle of the main plaza in the mall. We went and bought some candy while we were waiting for Fern to arrive.

The entrance to the movies was up a wide flight of stairs. We could see that there was a long line of people there already, waiting to buy tickets. There are five different screens. *Mayhem at Mindy's* was showing on Screen 1.

Fern arrived just after Pippa and I had paid for our candy.

'There was no one home all morning?' Fern said after I told her about Cindy. 'Are you sure you're dialling the right number?'

I just looked at her. I mean, Cindy and I have been best friends for *years*. I was hardly likely to have forgotten her number after all that time.

We walked up the stairs and joined on to the end of the movie line.

'Maybe their phone's out of order,' Pippa suggested as she handed round one of the candy bags.

'Maybe they've been abducted by aliens,' Fern said, chewing on some liquorice. 'You know the kind of thing. The whole house starts trembling and shaking.' She grabbed Pippa's shoulders and jerked her around. 'And then there's this brilliant white light and these tall skinny guys with huge heads and great big eyes come floating in. And the next thing the whole bunch of them are whooshed up to a spaceship and taken off to Mars.' Fern

27

stopped rattling Pippa round and nodded thoughtfully. 'That's my guess, anyway.'

'Maybe they just went away for the week-end,' Pippa said.

'Without telling us?' I said. 'Cindy wouldn't do that.' It was true. No way would Cindy have gone away for the weekend without letting me know. It was a real mystery.

'Here we go,' Fern said. The line had started moving, which meant the ticket booth must have opened.

We shuffled forwards as the line of people moved in through the entrance. There were a whole lot more people already in there.

'There's Judy MacWilliams,' Pippa said. She leaned on my shoulder and got right up on her tiptoes to see over people's backs. 'I wonder what movie she's going to see.'

I stretched my neck. Sure enough, I saw the rear view of Judy MacWilliams, leaning against a column. You couldn't mistake her. She's got this really long jet black hair that's cut straight halfway down her back. And, as usual, she was wearing skin-tight jeans and the smallest T-shirt in the world.

I'd just stuck my head out to take a look when she turned around. She stared straight at me for a couple of seconds. And then she smiled. That was weird. Why would Judy

MacWilliams *smile* at me? She usually totally ignored me.

And it was a pretty strange smile, too. A sneaky kind of smile.

We were almost at the ticket booth and I was just fishing in my pocket for some money, when I heard this really loud laugh from over where I'd seen Judy. It was *her* of course.

I couldn't help glancing round to see what was so funny.

My eyes nearly popped clean out of my head.

There were about ten people over by the entrance to Screen 3, where *Speedfreaks* was being shown. They all seemed to be eighth graders from my school. And Judy MacWilliams was hanging on some guy's arm and leaning all over him and gazing at him and laughing.

He had his back to me, but I knew right away who it was. No mistake. No *possible* mistake. The guy that Judy MacWilliams was heading into the movies with was James Baker.

Amanda's boyfriend! With Judy MacWilliams! Together! The two of them!

And Judy turned her head and looked straight at me and shot me a great big, triumphant smile. And I knew exactly what that smile meant.

'Next time you see Amanda,' Judy's smile meant, 'don't forget to tell her that you saw the two of us together!'

Chapter Four

'Hey, Mindy, where should I put these cakes?'

'Don't bother me with it now, Sharleen. Just put them on the end of the table.'

'OK, Mindy. Hey, it feels kind of wobbly. Oh! Help! The table's collapsed!'

'Sharleen! You are the dumbest girl in the entire school!'

I was nearly deafened by a yell of laughter from Fern. A mouthful of popcorn sprayed all over me. Pippa was giggling, too. In fact the entire audience had cracked up.

I'd been staring at the screen for half an hour without seeing a single thing. All I could see was Judy MacWilliams arm-in-arm with Amanda's James. And that *smile*! That awful, 'he's mine' smile!

Fern elbowed me in the ribs. She was almost doubled up with laughter. I was the only person in the movie theatre who wasn't laughing. Sharleen had slipped and was sitting amongst the cakes. And when the table had collapsed, a gooey pie of some sort had gone

31

flying through the air and smacked Mindy right in the face.

But the funniest film in the world wouldn't have even made me smile right then.

How could James *do* that? How could he take Judy MacWilliams to the movies while he was dating Amanda? And Judy had really enjoyed letting me see that they were together! Oh, she sure had!

So, now I guess I was meant to go right back home and tell Amanda. And then what would happen?

She'd go totally insane, that's what would happen.

But I had to tell her, didn't I? If James was two-timing her, the sooner Amanda knew about it the better.

Boy, did I have plenty to think about!

★ ★ ★

'That was great,' Pippa said as we came out of the movies. 'I haven't laughed so much in ages.'

'Film of the year!' Fern said. 'Definitely! Huh. Stacy? Film of the year, or what?'

'Yeah, great,' I said.

'So how come you weren't laughing?' Pippa asked.

I looked at them. 'I've got to tell you something,' I said. 'Something awful.'

32

We headed over to the food counter to get some burgers and milkshakes. Then we sat at a table and I told them what I'd seen.

'Are you sure it was James?' Fern asked.

'Of course I'm sure it was James,' I said. 'Do you think I'm blind or something?'

'OK, OK,' Fern said. 'Don't blow a fuse! I only asked.'

'Are you sure they were together?' Pippa asked. 'Maybe they were just next to each other in line by coincidence.'

'She was hanging onto his *arm*,' I said. I grabbed Pippa's arm with both hands. 'Like *this*! And she looked straight at me and gave me a great big grin. Don't you get it? She was really pleased that I saw her with him. Because she knew I'd tell Amanda.'

Pippa shook her head. 'Judy MacWilliams, of all people!'

'I know,' I said.

'Amanda and she absolutely *hate* each other,' Pippa said.

'I *know*,' I said.

'Amanda will be so mad you won't believe it,' Pippa said.

'I KNOW!' I said. 'Can you please stop telling me stuff I already know, and tell me what I'm going to do *now*?'

'You're not thinking of keeping it from her,

are you?' Fern asked. 'Stacy, you've got to tell her.'

'Maybe it's not what it looks like,' Pippa said. 'There could be some totally innocent explanation.'

'Like what?' I asked.

'Maybe James agreed to go out with Judy before he started going out with Amanda,' Pippa said. 'Maybe they arranged it weeks ago and he couldn't get out of it.'

'Puh-leeze!' Fern said. 'What kind of a guy arranges a date with someone, like, a *month* in advance, then starts dating a *different* girl, but still goes on the date with the first girl?' She gave me a knowing look. 'I'll tell you what kind of guy,' she said slowly. 'A cheap, two-timing, low-down, snake-in-the-grass-type guy, that's who.'

'I don't want to tell Amanda,' I said. 'I really don't. She'll be so hurt. She likes James a lot, I know she does.' I looked anxiously at them. 'How am I going to tell her?'

'Break it to her gently,' Pippa said.

'I've got it,' Fern said. 'You say, "Hands up everyone in the Allen family with a boyfriend who isn't two-timing them. Hey, Amanda, how come you're putting your hand up?" ' Fern grinned at me. 'That should do the trick.'

'Thanks a bunch, Fern,' I said. 'I can always rely on you to help out in a crisis.'

'Crisis-schmisis!' Fern said. 'Amanda should just say, "Hit the road, buddy, or I'll rearrange your face so good that you'll have to take your hat off to blow your nose!" '

'Don't listen to her,' Pippa said. 'What you need to do is sit Amanda down quietly somewhere and just tell her exactly what you saw. Then it's up to her to confront James.'

'And punch him in the kisser!' Fern added helpfully.

The person I really needed right then was Cindy. She wouldn't try to be funny like Fern, and her advice wasn't always guaranteed to get a person into trouble, like Pippa's. I was really missing Cindy right then!

'Maybe if James knew how much Amanda likes him,' I said after a long sip of milkshake and a long think. 'If he knew she really, really liked him lots and lots, then maybe he'd drop Judy again. Maybe this was his first date with Judy. And maybe it was Judy's idea. Maybe she chased *him*. Maybe he could be convinced that Amanda is a much nicer person than Judy.'

'And how do you do that?' Fern asked.

'I don't know right now,' I said. 'But I'll think of something.'

35

It was Sunday afternoon. I was in my room, and I'd come up with an idea. The way I saw it, James needed putting straight on one or two things. Like, he needed to know that Amanda was the girl for him. And he needed to know that Judy MacWilliams definitely *wasn't*.

I could tell Amanda what I'd seen. But knowing her, she'd just hit the roof and refuse ever to talk to him again. And I didn't want that to happen.

So somehow I had to get through to James and get him to drop Judy, without Amanda knowing anything about it.

And how was I going to do that? Simple! By writing an anonymous letter to James, telling him how much Amanda liked him. Smart, huh?

To make sure there was no way James could ever figure out whose writing it was, I wrote the whole letter in block capitals.

When I'd finished it I turned to read the letter out loud to Benjamin to see what he thought of it.

'Dear James,' I read. 'I am writing this to let you know that Amanda Allen likes you a whole lot. She likes you much better than someone else does. She would be upset if she couldn't go out with you any more. And you would not like going out with someone else because she is not a nice person. Best wishes. A friend.'

I looked at Benjamin.

'Well? What do you think? Pretty smart, huh?'

Benjamin was kind of busy with one of his mega-washes, but I could tell he thought my letter was OK.

I sat and looked at the letter while I chewed the end of my pen. There was something about it that was bugging me. It felt like it needed some kind of big finish. Something to convince James once and for all.

I wrote: 'P.S. Amanda is crazy about you and thinks you are totally wonderful and wants to be with you for ever and ever.'

Yeah! That would do it. That would stop him wanting to go out with Judy MacWilliams. I mean, what guy could resist being told he was totally wonderful?

Now all I needed to do was drop the letter off at James's house without being seen. I'd found out where he lived from Amanda's address book. It was only a couple of blocks away from Cindy's house, so I could ride over there, put the anonymous letter under James's door, and then go and see if there was any trace of Cindy or her family. I *still* hadn't

37

gotten any answer from Cindy's house on the phone.

'Mom,' I called down the basement stairs, 'I'm going to ride over to Cindy's.' Mom was down there working on some book which needed to be finished really quickly. Dad had taken Sam to the park for the afternoon.

'I thought there was no one home,' Mom called back.

'There might be by the time I get there,' I yelled. ''Bye.' Of course, I didn't mention my plan to stop by at James Baker's house first.

I was lucky. I managed to slide my anonymous letter under the front door to James's house without anyone spotting me. I'd put it in an envelope with *PRIVATE! FOR JAMES BAKER'S EYES ONLY* written on it in red magic marker.

I got back on my bike and headed off for Cindy's house. I rang the doorbell but there was no answer. I peered in through the windows. There was no sign of anyone.

I gave up. I couldn't think *where* they were. The whole thing was a total mystery to me. I mean, for all I knew Fern might have been right and they'd been abducted by aliens!

I was just climbing on my bike to go home when I heard a car toot its horn behind me. I looked around. It was *their* car.

Cindy's mom and dad were in the front and

Denny and Bob and Cindy were in the back. Denny and Bob are Cindy's twin kid brothers. Just don't *ask* me about them! They're awful!

They all waved to me as Mrs Spiegel turned the car into their driveway.

Denny was out of the car first. (Actually, it might have been Bob. I can't tell them apart without name tags.)

'We're going to California!' he yelled excitedly. 'We're going to go and live in California!'

I was still trying to take this in when Bob jumped out. (Or it might have been Denny.)

'We've been on an aeroplane,' he yelled at me. 'We've seen our new house and everything. It's totally brilliant.'

The twins raced up to the front door, pushing and shoving and arguing with each other like they always do.

Cindy got out of the car. She just stood in the driveway looking at me.

'Hi, Stacy,' she said.

'Hi,' I said back. And then we just stood there staring at each other and I couldn't think of a single thing to say.

Chapter Five

'How long have you known?' I asked Cindy. We were up in her room. Cindy was unpacking her bag and I was sitting on the bed, feeling like I'd just been hit by a truck.

'A couple of weeks,' she said quietly. She looked around at me. 'I *wanted* to tell you, but I couldn't think *how*.'

I guess I should explain.

About a month ago Cindy had told me that her mom had an interview for a new job. A job that would mean getting a whole lot more money. The only problem, Cindy told me, was that it was out of town. And not only out of town, but also out of Indiana. If her mom got the job it would mean the whole family relocating to San Diego. And San Diego is in California, which is hundreds and hundreds of miles away.

You can imagine how I felt about *that*! The best friend I've ever had in my entire life – *fifteen hundred miles away*??? No, thanks!

The thing is, Cindy never mentioned the

job again after that. I figured someone else had gotten it so I just breathed a sigh of relief and forgot all about it.

Up until today! Up until Denny and Bob had broken the news to me in that really *thoughtful* and *considerate* way.

'So, what were you planning on doing?' I said. 'Leaving me a goodbye note?' I guess I sounded angry and hurt, because Cindy just gave me a miserable look and didn't say anything.

Neither of us spoke. She finished unpacking and put her bag in the bottom of her closet.

'I bought you *this*,' Cindy mumbled. She shoved a small bundle of tissue paper into my hand.

I unwrapped it. It was a smooth round pebble painted to look like a smiling pig. I turned it over. On the back was a sticker. It said, *A Gift from San Diego*.

Cindy sat next to me on the bed.

'I didn't know how to tell you,' she said. 'I knew you'd be really upset. *I* don't want to go to California. It wasn't *my* idea at all. I'd much rather stay here with you and Pippa and Fern and Lucky.'

(Lucky is our jointly-owned pet puppy. He lives with Fern, but Pippa, Fern, Cindy and I own a quarter each.)

I sat there clutching my San Diego pebble

pig. If I looked the way Cindy looked, and if she felt the way I felt, then we had to be the two most miserable people in the entire world.

I swallowed hard. 'So,' I said. 'What's San Diego like?'

'Big,' Cindy said. 'And noisy.' She sighed. 'And too far away.'

★ ★ ★

I got home feeling pretty blue. Dad was just coming down the stairs with a pile of laundry.

'Hey, what's wrong, honey?' he asked as soon as he took a look at my face.

So I told him. We sat on the stairs and he gave me lots of hugs. And I cried a little. And Mom came out from the living room. And she sat on the stairs with us and gave me more hugs, which made me cry even more.

'You'll be able to write to each other,' Mom said. 'And call each other on the phone sometimes. And maybe you could even go visit her for a vacation. It won't be so bad, sweetie.'

'It won't be the same,' I said.

Mom gave me another rib-crushing hug. 'No,' she said, 'it won't be the same. But you'll still be friends. People don't stop being friends just because they move away from each other. Friends are still friends even if one of them goes to live as far away as *China*. Friendship doesn't count the miles.'

I sniffed and wiped a fistful of sleeve across my eyes.

'You ought to put that in a greetings card,' I said.

Mom smiled. 'You're right. I should. Friendship doesn't count the miles. That's pretty good, although I say so myself. What can I rhyme with miles, though?'

'Smiles,' Dad said.

Mom grinned. 'Yes. Smiles is perfect. Stacy? Think of a line that fits with "friendship doesn't count the miles", and ends with "smiles".'

'How about: I'll always think of you with smiles,' I said.

We went into the kitchen for some cherry pie and ice cream. Mom says she thinks best with a big slice of cherry pie. (I think best with chocolate chip cookies.)

We sat at the table and it wasn't long before we had the whole rhyme worked out.

Even though you're far away,
I think about you every day.
For friendship doesn't count the miles,
I'll always think of you with smiles.

'Now,' Mom said, 'what about making Cindy a special Bon Voyage card? You could get all her friends to write a message inside

43

and sign it, and you could write our rhyme in it as well.'

'I'm not too good at making things,' I reminded her.

'Amanda will help you, I'm sure,' Dad said. 'And I know a way of making it really special. You collect photos of all her friends and stick them in the card alongside their message. That way, she'll have photographs to remember you all by, so she'll never forget you.'

I sighed and sniffled a little. That sounded such a nice idea that it made me want to burst out crying again. 'I wish she wasn't going,' I said. 'I feel awful.'

Mom put her hand under my chin and lifted my face up so I was looking into her eyes.

'You mustn't let Cindy know you feel like that,' she said.

I frowned. 'Why not?'

'Well, just think how Cindy must be feeling,' Mom said. 'She's going to have to leave all her friends, her school, everything. That's going to be hard enough for her, without you making it worse by being sad.'

'I can't help being sad,' I said.

'We know, honey,' Dad said. 'What your mom means is that Cindy will need you and Pippa and Fern and everyone to help keep her cheerful. You've got to help her think that it's a really big adventure.'

'That's right,' Mom added. 'It is an adventure. Cindy will be like a *scout*, sending back reports of all the new things she finds. And maybe you could even publish her letters in the school magazine. *Letters from the West Coast. By our roving reporter, Cindy Spiegel.* How does that sound?'

'And I guess she won't be all that far from Hollywood,' I said. 'She could send photos of herself with Eddie Eden. He lives in Hollywood. Amanda will be so jealous!'

Dad ruffled my hair. 'Are you feeling a little more cheerful, now, Snookie-poos?'

'Yeah, thanks, I guess I am,' I said. 'A *little* more cheerful. But, Dad?'

'Yes, honey?'

'Will you do me a really big favour?'

'Sure. Anything for my little sweetiepie.'

'Will you stop calling me *Snookie-poos*?' I said. 'Sweetiepie, I can handle. Honeybunch, I can handle. But *Snookie-poos* is just too much!'

Mom and Dad both laughed, which kind of surprised me, because I really *meant* it!

★ ★ ★

Amanda arrived home late that evening. Cheryl's dad dropped her off around six

45

o'clock. I expected her to be dead tired after two whole days of leaping around kicking her legs in the air, waving pop-poms around and going 'Rah! Rah! Rah! We are the best! Rah! Rah! Rah! Better than the rest!' and all that kind of thing.

Not Amanda. She started talking from the moment she hit the front door mat and she didn't stop for breath until Mom brought her in a slice of pizza.

'Oh, great,' she said, grabbing the pizza and eating it in about three mouthfuls. 'I was absolutely starving.'

'Didn't they feed you?' Dad asked, watching in amazement as the pizza slice vanished.

'Oh, sure,' Amanda mumbled with her mouth crammed full. 'But you use up so much *energy*. I can't *tell* you!' Which was a pretty strange thing for her to say, considering that she'd *been* telling us non-stop for the past half an hour.

Amanda handed Mom the empty plate.

'Is there any more?' Amanda asked.

'Sure,' Mom said with a grin. 'I'll put some more in the oven.'

By the end of the evening we must have been told in detail about every single thing Amanda had done over the entire weekend.

And she had managed to eat *four* slices of pizza at the same time.

Eventually Amanda ran out of things to tell us.

'I'll just go call James,' she said. 'To let him know I'm back.'

'Not at this time of night you won't,' Mom said. 'Have you taken a look at the clock recently?'

It was way past my usual bedtime. Amanda had been talking for *hours*!

'Oh, I didn't realize,' Amanda said. 'But I'm too excited to sleep. We've got a whole bunch of new moves to practise next week. Let me show you this really good one.'

'Not *now*,' Mom said. 'Show us tomorrow, honey. And, Stacy? I want you in bed and fast asleep in *ten* minutes. Got me?'

'Sure thing,' I said.

I washed and brushed my teeth and changed into my pyjamas. I could hear Amanda moving around in her room. I could feel this *urge* building up inside me. An urge to tell her all about James and Judy, and to tell her that I'd put a letter under James's door, telling him he should stick with *her* and forget all about Judy Mac-creep-face-Williams.

I knew really that I couldn't tell her, but it was driving me crazy that she didn't know the

47

big favour I'd done her with that anonymous letter. I had to tell her *something* or I'd go crazy.

I padded along the hallway to her room.

She was emptying out her bag in typical Amanda-fashion, by turning it upside down so everything fell out onto the floor. Then she picked up the stuff she wanted right away and kicked the rest into the corners. No wonder her room was like a landfill site!

'Cindy's going to go and live in California,' I told Amanda.

Amanda stopped and looked at me. 'Wow! Cool! How come?'

'Her mom's got a job out there.'

'California!' Amanda said in a dreamy voice. 'Do you think we'll be able to go visit her on vacations? The other guys would be so green when I came back and showed them my tan.'

'She's my best friend!' I said pretty loudly. Amanda didn't seem to understand what I was telling her. 'My best friend is going to go and live hundreds of miles away!'

'She's so lucky.' Amanda sighed, and I could tell that her head was full of visions of long sandy beaches and surf and sunshine. 'Why couldn't Dad have gotten a job some-where fabulous like that, instead of up *north*?'

'Well, thanks for your *sympathy*, Amanda,'

I said. 'Remind me to be just as sympathetic back if Cheryl ever leaves town. Although if I had a best friend like Cheryl Ruddick, California wouldn't be far enough for her to go! And that's the last time I ever do you any favours!'

Amanda just looked at me. 'What favours?' she said. 'What are you talking about?'

Oops! I almost let the cat out of the bag, there.

'No favours at all,' I said. 'I . . . I meant . . . if I'd been *planning* on doing you any favours at all ever, then I wouldn't now. So there!'

I stormed out and went back to my own room. I left the door open a little so Benjamin could come and go if he wanted to. (Benjamin hates closed doors.)

I got into bed and switched off the light. Sometimes I just couldn't *believe* my sister! I'd been worrying about her like crazy ever since I'd seen James and Judy at the movies yesterday afternoon. But when I go looking for just a *tiny* piece of sympathy or concern from her when I tell her my best friend is leaving town, all she can think about is the chance for her to be invited over to get a tan!

I'll tell you, there are times when I don't know why I like Amanda *at all*!

Chapter Six

Next morning at breakfast I had mentioned to Mom exactly how sympathetic and understanding my self-centred sister had been when I'd told her the news about Cindy.

'I guess she was just tired,' Mom had said. 'Did you ask her about helping with the Bon Voyage card?'

'No, I didn't,' I'd said. 'And I'm not going to. I don't need her help.'

Mom had just looked at me without saying anything.

I ignored Amanda when she came down for breakfast. I didn't stick my tongue out at her or anything like that. I just behaved as if she wasn't there.

I didn't even wait for her when I heard Mom call her back as we were heading out of the front door.

Amanda caught up with me just as the school bus was coming along.

'Are you upset with me?' she asked as we

got on the bus. 'You were being weird all through breakfast.'

'Why should I be upset with you?' I said in a really dignified and grown up way. 'What could *you* do to upset me?'

Usually Amanda went straight to the back to sit with her friends, but today she grabbed me and pulled me down in a seat near the front.

'Mom says to say sorry for being so unsympathetic last night,' Amanda said. '*She* said I upset you.' She looked closely at me. 'Did I upset you?'

'No more than usual,' I said stiffly. 'A person gets used to it after a while.'

'Loosen up, Stacy,' Amanda said. 'I told you I was sorry. What more do you want? A written apology?'

'You haven't told me you're sorry at all,' I said. 'All you've said is that Mom *told* you to say you were sorry. What kind of an apology is that?'

Amanda gazed out of the window for a couple of blocks. I could see she was trying to work this out.

'OK,' she said after a while. 'I've thought about it, right? And I *am* sorry that Cindy is leaving. I know you really love her, and I know you'll be upset when she goes. Now, do you want me to help with the going away card Mom told me about?'

'You don't *have* to,' I said.

'I know I don't *have* to,' Amanda said. 'I'm offering to help. I'm not getting down on my bended knees about it, Stacy. The offer's there. Take it or leave it.'

'I'll take it,' I said. 'Thanks.'

'Right,' she got up. 'Give me the details sometime. See you.' She headed down to the back of the bus and I went to sit next to Fern and break the news about Cindy.

'So her mom *did* get the job,' Fern said after I'd filled her in about the Big Move. 'Wow, Cindy sure kept *that* quiet. Why didn't she tell us?'

'She thought we'd be upset, I guess,' I said.

'Hmm,' Fern said. 'I guess we'll miss her, huh?'

'Kind of,' I sighed.

'There'll only be the three of us,' Fern said. She gave me a long, thoughtful look. 'You know,' she said. 'I don't know whether to feel really sad that she's going to be leaving, or really excited for her that she'll be living in California.'

'I guess I feel *both*,' I said. 'Excited and sad at the same time. It's kind of confusing.'

Then I told Fern about the Bon Voyage

card idea, with photos of all her friends and special messages.

'It'll have to be a big card,' Fern said.

I smiled. 'It sure will. The biggest Bon Voyage card *ever*!'

We met up with Pippa outside the main entrance to the school. We dragged her off to a quiet corner so we wouldn't be interrupted by Cindy.

Pippa felt the same about it as Fern and I did. It was like part of each of us couldn't really believe it was true. Like it was impossible to imagine Cindy not being around. And part of us felt sad because we'd miss her so much. And then *another* part was really amazed that one of us was going to be living in California.

'The way I see it,' Pippa said, 'they won't be leaving for *months*. I mean, Mrs Spiegel will have to quit her old job. They'll have to sell the house. And they'll have to find a new school for Cindy to go to in San Diego.' She nodded knowingly. 'Trust me,' she said. 'It'll be three months, at least.'

*   *   *

I had a few minutes spare before classes, so I went looking for Amanda. Now I'd had time to discuss it with Pippa and Fern, I thought

I'd let Amanda know about our ideas for Cindy's Bon Voyage card.

The James and Judy problem was still clomping around inside my head like a rhino with heavy boots on. I couldn't get Judy's smile out of my mind! I just hoped that my letter had done the trick and that I'd see James and Amanda back together sometime today.

Amanda was in the eighth grade locker hall-way, huddled in a corner with Cheryl, Natalie and Rachel.

All I could hear as I walked towards them was Cheryl's hyena laugh and Natalie's squeaky voice saying, 'His name is Brandon De Ville, and he looks so *cool*!'

'Where's he from?' Amanda asked.

Bimbo Conversation Topics.
1.   Hairdos.
2.   Clothes.
3.   Pop Stars/Film Stars.
4.   Boys.
5.   Nothing Else.

At a wild guess, I'd say they were on topic number 4.

'Well,' Natalie squeaked, 'Brenda Bansini said that she heard he was *expelled* from his last school for telling the principal to get lost after he'd missed some detention he'd been given for smoking.'

'It was worse than that, according to Carol Nuncarrow,' Cheryl said. 'According to Carol he was expelled for . . .' She lowered her voice and the other three Bimbo heads bent forward to listen like they were in a football huddle.

There was a kind of breathless 'Oooh!' from all of them.

'Oh, wow!' Amanda said. 'He didn't! That's so cool!'

'I'd like to see any of the boys in this school do something like that,' Rachel said.

'Excuse me,' I said. There was no point in me hanging around politely until there was a break in the conversation. I could be waiting all day. 'Amanda? Can I have a word with you?'

She frowned at me. 'Not now, Stacy,' she said. 'I'm busy.'

'No, you're not,' I said. 'You're just beating your gums about some boy.'

I guess I should have been a little more polite, but that doesn't excuse Amanda for telling me to get lost in *quite* such a rude way!

'I'll tell Mom what you just called me,' I yelled after them as the four Bimbos headed down the hallway to get another look at this new boy they were talking about.

'She'll make you wash your mouth out with soap!' I hollered as the swing doors went flap-flap-flap behind them.

★   ★   ★

I met up with Cindy in homeroom. Fern and Pippa were already there and Ms Fenwick was about to take the roll.

I sat next to Cindy.

'I've got a guide book,' Cindy whispered, passing me a small colourful book under the desk. Ms Fenwick doesn't like us to chat or do anything while she's trying to see who's there and who's missing, because she says it distracts her. So you have to be kind of sneaky if you want to pass information to one another.

I took a look at the booklet. It had a photo of a beach on the front, and a yellow cartoon sun with a big grin. 'CALIFORNIA!' was written in big yellow and red letters.

'Looks good,' I whispered. I'd decided to take my mom's advice, and be really *positive* about Cindy's move. Then I remembered what Pippa had said earlier. I guess I really ought to have asked Cindy when I first heard the news, but I hadn't.

'When are you supposed to be leaving?' I whispered.

'Stacy, are you talking?'

Sheesh! Ms Fenwick has ears like a bat sometimes.

'No, I mean, yes,' I said.

'Well, please, don't,' Ms Fenwick said. 'It's very distracting.'

What did I tell you?

Actually, I really like Ms Fenwick, even though she's kind of strict with us.

I didn't get another chance to talk to Cindy until after homeroom.

'Two weeks,' she said.

I looked at her.

'Two weeks?' I repeated. 'Two weeks *what*?'

'You asked when we were leaving,' Cindy said. 'In two weeks.'

'You're kidding?'

'Nope.'

I turned around in my seat to where Pippa and Fern were sitting right behind us.

'I should have known you'd get it wrong!' I said, glaring at Pippa.

'What?' Pippa asked. 'What have I done now?'

'Cindy's leaving in *two weeks*!' I said. 'Not three months.'

Pippa stared at her. 'How can you *do* that?' she asked. 'When Mom and I moved to our place, it took forever, and we were only moving across town.' I ought to mention, here, that Pippa's mom and dad are divorced and Pippa lives with her mom.

'My mom starts her new job in two weeks,' Cindy said. 'At first she was going to go on ahead and we were going to follow after a few weeks. But then Uncle Tony said he'd handle selling our house for us, and Mom and Dad had already found a house for us in San Diego which we can move into as soon as we like.' Cindy took a big breath. 'And so Dad resigned from his job two weeks ago and the moving company is booked, and the aeroplane tickets have been bought and Mom's sent a letter to the school, and we've all got places in a school in San Diego.' Cindy looked anxiously at us. 'And I feel like I'm on some kind of roller-coaster. I keep hoping I'll wake up and everything will be back to normal.'

I gave her a reassuring hug and by then it was time for class.

Two weeks? Two weeks and Cindy would be gone. That's the kind of idea that takes a while to get used to.

* * *

I decided I'd better get on Amanda's case again about Cindy's card. I went on an Amanda hunt at break. I found Natalie Smith gazing at herself in a hand mirror and tweaking her long ash-blonde hair. That girl is *always* messing with her hair. It grows all the way down to her backside and she must spend half her life brushing it and making sure it looks perfect.

'Hmm,' I said, giving her hair a close look. 'Plenty of split ends, there, Nat, I think you're going to need to cut it all off.'

'I do not have split ends!' Natalie squeaked. 'And don't call me Nat!'

I made scissors movements with my fingers and grinned.

'Seen Amanda?' I asked.

Natalie grabbed a fistful of hair and started examining it. 'I do not have split ends,' she muttered, peering at her hair. 'I do *not*!'

'Hello!' I said. 'Earth to Natalie. Have you seen Amanda?'

'No. Get lost, Stacy!'

It took me about ten minutes to finally nail Amanda down.

I came around a corner and found her standing in the front hall talking to some boy. A boy I hadn't seen before. And Amanda was batting her eyelids and flashing her biggest smiles and giggling like a total bozo.

In other words, Amanda was *flirting* with this guy! Flirting right out there in full view!

All it needed was for James to see them and that'd be one promising relationship down the tubes.

Chapter Seven

There were times when it felt like I was the only person who was taking the relationship between my big sister and James Baker *seriously*!

Amanda spent a weekend away at camp. What did James do? Did he sit at home with a picture of her, counting the hours until she got back? Heck, no! He was out with Judy MacWilliams almost before Amanda hit the edge of town.

And what did she do between classes on her first day back? Did she run off to find James to tell him how much she missed him? No, she was hanging around in the hall, flapping her eyelashes and sparkling her teeth like a *flirt-monster* from the planet Bimbo with some totally *other* guy!

And who *was* this guy? I took a good look at him. He had longish black hair, parted in the middle and hanging over his face. And he was wearing shades and a black leather jacket. And he was leaning against the wall with his hands in his pockets like he was some kind of bad dude gangster. Not exactly a Boy Scout.

'Sorry,' Amanda was saying as I came around the corner. 'I don't think I can do that, Brandon. My boyfriend might not like it.'

Brandon! Now I knew who he was. He was the new guy that the Bimbos had been talking about earlier. Brandon De Ville. The *bad* boy who had been expelled from his last school.

Brandon came out with the slickest, snakiest smile you could imagine. 'Your boyfriend is a loser,' he said.

'You don't even know who my boyfriend is,' Amanda said.

'I don't need to,' Brandon said. 'I know he's a loser, because you're coming to the dance with *me* on Friday, and he's going to be sitting at home sorting his stamp collection.' He cocked a finger at her like he was firing a gun. 'And that's a *fact*, Amanda.'

Then he peeled himself off the wall and walked off. Amanda just stood there, clutching her books against herself and staring after him. She looked kind of breathless.

'Ew!' I said as I came up to her. 'Who was *that*?'

'Brandon,' Amanda breathed. 'Brandon De Ville.'

'What kind of an idiot wears sunglasses

indoors?' I said. 'And what's with the leather jacket? Was he cold or something?'

Amanda didn't say anything.

'What did he want with you?' I asked. 'Hello! Amanda, are you in there?'

'Huh?' Finally she looked at me. 'Oh, Stacy. Hi. What do you want?'

'Are you OK?' I asked. She didn't seem OK. She seemed like her brain had just closed down for the day.

'Yeah, I'm fine.'

'So, what did *he* want?'

'He wanted me to go to the dance with him,' Amanda said.

The dance. The big eighth grade dance. It was being held on Friday night in the school hall.

'Well!' I said, 'I hope you told him where to get off. I hope you told him you're going with your boyfriend.'

'Uh, I think I did,' Amanda said.

'Well, did you or didn't you?' I asked. 'And what was that stuff about James being a loser? Where does that creep get off, saying things like that!'

Amanda stared straight through me as if she hadn't heard a word I'd said.

'Uh, I need to go, Stacy,' she said. 'I'll see you later.'

I followed her as she wandered off.

'I want to talk to you about Cindy's card,' I said. 'Dad had this idea of sticking photos of all her friends in it. And Mom and I wrote this really good poem, so we've got the inside figured out. What I want you to do is to design something for the front.'

'Yeah,' Amanda said. 'You do that.'

I stared at her. '*You do that*? What are you talking about?'

'Whatever you said.'

I grabbed her arm and she turned to look at me.

'Have you been listening to me?' I said.

'Sure. You want me to take some photos of Cindy.'

'No! No! No! I'll sort the photos out. I want you to design something brilliant for the front of the card.'

'Fine,' Amanda said. She still didn't sound like she was on the same planet as me. 'I've got it. Stacy. Leave it with me. I'll come up with something really Brandon for the front.'

'Something really *what*?' I said.

'Brilliant.'

'You said *Brandon*,' I told her.

'I did not,' Amanda said. 'I said brilliant. Can I have my arm back, Stacy?'

I let go of her and she walked off.

My sister acts like her brain is in orbit at the best of times. But for the last five minutes

63

she'd been behaving like her brain had just passed Jupiter and was heading into deep space.

* * *

The four of us were sitting at our favourite table in the cafeteria having our lunch.

We were all feeling kind of gloomy, thanks to Pippa.

When we'd first brought our plates over here, Pippa had said, 'There'll be an empty seat here in two weeks' time.'

That had *really* cheered us all up big time!

Cindy sighed and wiggled her spoon around in her yoghurt, fishing for blueberries.

Pippa sighed and sat there folding her napkin into a smaller and smaller square.

I sighed and gazed out of the window, thinking about all the good times I'd had with Cindy.

Fern blew noisy bubbles in her orange juice through her straw. We all looked at her.

'Sorry,' she said. 'The silence was driving me crazy.'

I looked around the cafeteria and caught sight of James and a couple of his friends making their way through the tables with their trays.

I was desperate to know what he'd thought

of the letter I'd written. But I could hardly go up to him and *ask*.

On the other hand, if I just sat there and did nothing, I was going to *explode* with curiosity.

'I'm just going to have a quick word with James,' I told the others. I hadn't mentioned the letter to them. I had a feeling they might tell me it was a bad idea and that I shouldn't have interferred. And I didn't really need to be told *that* now that it was too late to do anything about it.

I made my way over to the table where James and his friends had just sat down.

'Hi, James,' I said.

He looked up at me. 'Oh, hi.'

'Have you seen Amanda?' I asked.

'No.' He gave me a very strange look. He stood up and took me to one side. 'Listen, Stacy,' he said really quietly, 'has she said anything to you about me?'

I looked at him. 'Like what?'

'Uh, I don't know.' He looked around, as if checking that no one could overhear us. 'About how she *feels* about me?'

Hey, maybe he had a guilty conscience about going to the movies with Judy. Maybe Judy had told him I was there, and *now* he was checking to see if I'd told Amanda, and whether she totally hated him now.

'As far as I know, she likes you just as much

65

as she ever did,' I said. 'Why?' Is there some reason why she *wouldn't* like you so much any more?'

'Not that I know of,' he said.

'How was the *movie*?' I asked.

'The movie?' James said. 'Oh! The *movie*. It was fine.' Whoo! Talk about cool as a cucumber. 'But, the thing is, I was out all day Sunday, and when I got home I found a letter on the hall mat, and . . . oh!' He looked over my shoulder and suddenly seemed embarrassed and nervous. 'Never mind, Stacy,' he mumbled. 'Forget I mentioned it. I've got to go.'

And he zipped off among the tables and vanished through the exit. And he hadn't even touched his lunch.

'Where'd he go?' It was Amanda. She'd come up behind me. James must have seen her. He'd run off because he didn't want to speak to her. I guess he thought I'd told her about J.U.D.Y. and he was expecting to get chewed out about it.

'I wanted to talk to him,' Amanda said. 'Didn't he *see* me?'

'I guess not,' I said.

'What were you talking about?' Amanda asked.

'Nothing.'

'Nothing?' Amanda put her hands on her

66

hips. 'How can you have been talking about *nothing*?'

'It's easy,' I said. 'You should know. You and Cheryl do it all the time.'

Amanda couldn't have been listening, or she'd have had something to say about that crack.

'If I didn't know better,' she said, staring towards the exit, and sounding as if she was talking to herself, 'I'd almost think he was *avoiding* me. This is the third time today that he's done this. Am I wearing the wrong deodorant, or something?'

'Beats me,' I said, and I headed back to the guys, leaving her standing there looking very puzzled.

At least I knew one thing now. James had gotten my letter.

But I was beginning to think that maybe I should have just *told* him that I'd seen him with Judy, but that I wouldn't tell if he promised never to two-time Amanda again. Yeah, maybe that anonymous letter wasn't the *perfect* solution after all.

The problem was that if I came clean with him now, and told him that I'd written the letter, he'd probably think I was a total pea-brained idiot.

Maybe I shouldn't have gotten involved after all.

It was *all* Pippa's fault! She told me I shouldn't interfere, so *naturally* I did the opposite to what she said. Trust Pippa to be *right* for the first time in her entire life!

Chapter Eight

After school we all went back to Cindy's house for a while. We didn't usually spend much time at Cindy's house because Denny and Bob were always such a pain. But Cindy had told us they'd be out for a couple of hours, so it was safe.

Things already looked different. The downstairs back room was full of cardboard boxes, and when we arrived Cindy's grandmother was wrapping the best china in tissue paper and carefully packing it away.

'You girls go get yourselves something to eat,' she said. 'There's plenty in the fridge.'

'What will you do when Cindy and her mom and dad and Denny and Bob are gone?' Fern asked Cindy's grandmother. Cindy had always told us that her grandmother *lived* for the afternoons when she went round there to keep an eye on Cindy and the twins until their dad got home from work.

I thought it was kind of tactless of Fern to ask a question like that. But then Fern never was the most tactful person in the entire world.

'I guess I'll find something to pass the time,' Cindy's grandmother said with a smile, but I could tell she wasn't looking forward to it at all.

The real shock came when we went into Cindy's room. *That's* when it really hit home! One of the cardboard boxes was in a corner, and loads of Cindy's things were already packed away. Her doll collection that had filled five shelves. All her books and board games. She'd even taken all the posters and pictures down off the walls.

The pale patches on the paint made me feel all hollow inside.

The only thing left on the wall was a calendar over her bed. A big calendar with a different cat photo for every month. I'd given it to her for Christmas. I'd never *dreamed* that by the time she got to next Christmas, she'd be hundreds of miles away.

The Saturday in two weeks' time was ringed with red and Cindy had written a countdown over the next twelve days.

Cindy sat on her bed.

'I packed most of my things on Sunday night,' she said. 'I couldn't sleep.'

'Isn't it going to be weird, living out of a box for the next two weeks?' Fern asked.

Cindy sighed. 'I guess,' she said. 'But not half so weird as living in San Diego without all of you.'

We sat around, munching our food and not saying much.

'Let's play something,' Pippa said. 'What about Monopoly?'

We all just looked at her.

'Come on, you guys,' she said, jumping up. 'We've got to do something to cheer ourselves up.'

'I packed all my games,' Cindy said. 'I think Monopoly is right at the bottom of the box. Sorry.'

'Great!' Pippa said, collapsing back onto the floor. 'Just great. So, what are we going to do?'

'We could start thinking about who's going to replace Cindy in the gang,' Fern said.

She saw the look of total horror on all our faces.

'Joke, guys,' she said. She gave us a sickly grin. 'It was just a joke.'

We ended up downstairs helping Cindy's grandmother pack the china and glassware from the living room display cabinet. When Cindy's mom got back from the swimming pool with Denny and Bob we decided it was time to go home.

I found Mom having a quiet half-hour in

the living room. She had her needlepoint stuff out. She'd been working on the needlepoint for *years*. It was a big tree with lots of animal heads sticking out through the leaves. The name of the needlepoint was the Tree of Life.

Sam was lying fast asleep on the couch next to her, so I just crept in and sat on the floor and had a look at the picture of how the tree was supposed to look when it was finished. Mom had done maybe two thirds of it. Right then she was sewing a bird that was flying above the tree.

'Did you speak to Amanda about Cindy's card?' Mom asked.

'Yes,' I said. 'She said she'd do it, but I don't think she was really listening to what I was telling her. Mom?'

'Yes, honey?'

'When you and Dad were going out,' I asked, 'did either of you go out with other people at the same time?'

I was trying to figure whether it was OK for James to take Judy out while he was going out with Amanda. It didn't seem to me like an OK thing to do at *all*, but then I'm only ten, so what do I know about things like that?'

'Let me think,' Mom said. 'I don't think your dad was seeing anyone else. But I had a little problem with a boy called Bobby Martin, who was my boyfriend at the time. Bobby and your dad overlapped a little, so I guess I was going out with two boys at once for a few weeks.' She smiled. 'But then I realized that your dad was *the one*, so I had to tell Bobby I couldn't see him any more.'

'So you were still seeing this Bobby guy for a couple of weeks?'

'Uh-huh,' Mom nodded. She grinned. 'Why, honey? Do you have two boyfriends on hold right now?'

'Mom!!!'

I wasn't sure that Mom's answer had helped a whole bunch. As far as I knew, James hadn't been dating Judy before he started going out with Amanda. But maybe he *had*. Or maybe it was the *other way around*. Maybe he was losing interest in Amanda, and maybe what I saw on Saturday was his first date with Judy. And maybe he'd decided Judy was *the one*.

Poor Amanda! In the dumpster because of Judy MacWilliams. That had to be my sister's ultimate nightmare.

I got up off the floor and went upstairs. Whatever happened about James I wanted Amanda to know that I'd be there for her!

I knocked on her door. I heard a miserable kind of 'hruumph' noise from inside. I took that for a 'come in' and I opened the door. Amanda was lying on the floor with her hands behind her head, just staring up at the ceiling with a totally fed up look on her face. She was still in her school clothes, which was unusual. She normally took them off as soon as she got home.

'Hi, there,' I said cheerfully. 'I was walking past your door, and I thought to myself, hey, I wonder how Amanda is. I think I'll just knock on her door and say, hi.'

Amanda looked at me. 'I'm not in the mood,' she said. 'I just want to be left alone, OK?'

I looked at her. 'Is it James?'

'Is what James?'

'*It*,' I said. 'The *it* that's upset you. Is it something James had done? Or ... uh ... something that someone *told* you James has done?' I gave her my best caring-sister look. 'Do you want to talk about it?'

'No, I don't!'

'OK.'

Amanda sat up. 'I just don't get it,' she said. 'Maybe I'm imagining things, but it's like he's been avoiding me all day. I'll walk into a room, and he walks straight out. And the one time I managed to corner him, he said he was in a real hurry and that he'd meet me after school. But he never turned up. And when I called him at home his sister said he wasn't there.' Amanda banged both fists down on the floor. 'I want to know what's going on!'

Should I tell her? Was this the time to come clean about what I'd seen?

The problem was, how would Amanda react?

THE SHATTERED HEART
A tragedy of lost love.
by STACY ALLEN

(We join the action in the final moments of the last act.)

THE SCENE: Amanda's bedroom. Amanda is lying on her bed in a distressed state. Stacy stands by the bed. She has some appalling news for Amanda.

STACY: I have some appalling news for you, Amanda. Prepare yourself for the worst! I saw your beau, James Baker, in the arms of that scarlet woman, Judy MacWilliams.

AMANDA: (*Hysterically*) Oh, no! How could he! And with *her* of all women! The brutal monster! He has broken my heart into a thousand pieces and scattered it in the burning desert of my loneliness! I shall never love again! Leave me, leave me, my sister. All is lost!

Amanda pulls a small pearl-handled revolver from between her heaving bosoms.

Stacy recoils with a shocked gasp.

STACY: (*Shocked*) Gasp!

AMANDA: Oh, James! James! How could you do this to me? I shall end it all! I shall shoot myself right here where I sit!

STACY: No, Amanda! Don't shoot yourself right there where you sit! It would be very painful.

Stacy leaps forward and wrestles the gun from her half-crazed sister's hands. Amanda collapses onto the bed.

AMANDA: If I am not to be allowed to take the easy way out, then I shall spend the rest of my days in a convent! And I wish only this: that Judy MacWilliams breaks out in zits and develops an incurable overbite and fat ankles! Farewell, cruel world!

CURTAIN

Well, maybe not. (Especially not the part about the heaving bosoms. Amanda does *have* boobs, but she's got a long way to go before they start *heaving*.)

But she would be really upset. And I really, really didn't want to have to be the one to tell her.

I made a quick decision. I'd give it one more day. If things weren't OK with Amanda and James by this time tomorrow, I'd tell Mom about James and Judy. And then Mom could break the news to Amanda.

OK, so it wasn't very *brave* of me, but I was using all my bravery to stay cheerful in front of Cindy.

The way things worked out, I didn't have to tell Mom the news after all.

Amanda found out all by herself!

Chapter Nine

We were on the bus to school the next morning. I'd finally cornered Amanda into discussing Cindy's Bon Voyage card.

'OK,' Amanda said. 'You can have artistic or you can have slushy. You tell me which.'

'I'm not sure,' I said. 'Give me some examples.'

'Artistic would be something like, uhh . . .' Amanda's eyes narrowed and she stuck her tongue out like she did when she thought artistic thoughts. 'Like a golden leaf in fall. A single brown leaf on a cream background. Or maybe a trail of leaves going like *that* across the front.' She made a swooping movement with her arm. 'That would be totally sophisticated and artistic.'

I looked uncertainly at her. It sounded kind of dull to me. 'And slushy?'

'Oh, you know,' Amanda said with a shrug. 'Puppy dogs, big red hearts, flowers, kittens, balloons, streamers. *That* kind of stuff.'

'Sounds good,' I said. 'I think Cindy would prefer slushy, if it's all the same to you.'

Amanda sighed. 'So, what do you want? Kittens? Puppies? Flowers? Hearts?'

I grinned. 'All of them, please. And could you throw in a few stars and some birds? Oh, and you could do drawings of me and Fern and Pippa waving goodbye. And maybe a drawing of Four Corners and an aeroplane with Cindy and her folks in it, and a drawing of a beach where the aeroplane is heading. You know, a Californian-type beach.'

'And maybe a few surfers?' Amanda said.

'Yeah, great.'

'And sharks,' Amanda said sharply. 'A whole bunch of sharks! And Cindy in the water, being chomped up by them!'

I looked at her. I could tell she was getting annoyed. 'I was only trying to give you some ideas,' I said.

She patted me on the head in a way that would normally have really irritated me. 'You stick to what you're good at, Stacy, and leave me to the artistic stuff. OK?'

'Whatever you say, Amanda,' I replied.

The bus came to a stop outside our school and we all made the usual crazy rush for the doors.

'*Oof*! You'd think people would – *urgh*! –

grow out of this kind of behaviour!' I yelled as I elbowed my way out. '*Ugg* – excuse *me*!'

'Amanda-a-a-a!' It was a shriek like a fire alarm going off. Cheryl came racing up to Amanda with eyes like dinner plates and with this totally *appalled* expression on her face.

Amanda nearly jumped out of her socks as Cheryl grabbed hold of her.

'I don't know how to tell you,' she gabbled. 'It's awful!'

'What?' Amanda gasped, looking really alarmed. 'What happened?'

'It might not be true,' Cheryl burbled. 'I don't know if it's true. It might be a complete *lie*!'

'*What?*' Amanda hollered.

Cheryl took a deep breath. 'I was told,' she said slowly, 'that *James* is going out with Judy MacWiliams.'

Amanda went white. I mean, *really*! White as a sheet of paper!

'James *Baker*,' Cheryl said, as if she thought Amanda hadn't realized which James she was talking about. '*Your* James!'

'That's a lie!' Amanda said. 'Who told you that? Who's going around saying things like that?'

'Natalie told me, and Brenda told her. And Brenda got it straight from Maddie Fischer.'

Maddie Fischer was Judy's horrible, slimy

sidekick. They were always together, as if Maddie was Judy's pet warthog, or something.

'Maddie's a liar!' Amanda said. 'I wouldn't trust her one bit!'

'I'm only telling you what Natalie told me,' Cheryl said. 'According to what Maddie told Brenda, James and Judy went to the movies together last Saturday afternoon. And Maddie said they sat in the back row and *smooched* all the way through!'

'Wait till I get my hands on that lying toad Maddie Fischer!' Amanda growled.

'But they *were* together!' Cheryl said. She turned and looked straight at me. 'Weren't they, Stacy?'

Gulp!

Amanda turned on her heel and stared at me with a look on her face that would have stopped a stampeding herd of buffalo.

'Well?' she said.

Help! Get me out of this!

'I – I wasn't sure it was James,' I stammered. 'I only saw him from behind. It might have been someone else. Someone completely different. Someone who only looks like James . . . uh, from behind.'

'Someone who looked like James from behind?' Amanda said slowly.

I nodded. 'That's right. There must be

plenty of guys around who look *exactly* like James from behind.'

'What was he wearing?'

'Uh, jeans and a brown jacket.'

'A brown jacket like the one James wears?' Amanda said.

'Possibly,' I said.

'Was it or wasn't it?' Amanda snapped.

'It was the same sort of jacket,' I said. 'But it's hardly one of a kind. There must be plenty of guys who have jackets like that.'

Amanda took hold of my collar and slowly pulled me towards her until our noses were about half an inch apart.

'So, this guy looked *exactly* like James, and was wearing clothes *exactly* like James wears.'

'From behind,' I reminded her. 'Only from behind.'

'And you saw him at the movies last Saturday with Judy MacWilliams.'

'No!' I said. 'I didn't. That's not true. They were in the lobby waiting in line for *Speedfreaks*. And all I saw was Judy clinging onto some guy who looked like James. And she saw me and grinned. But I didn't see them *in* the movies. And I sure didn't see them smooching!'

'You saw Judy MacWillliams all over a guy who looked exactly like James,' Amanda's voice got more and more shrill, 'lining up to see *exactly* the same movie James said he was going to see, at exactly the time he was going to see it. And you didn't mention it to me because you thought it might be *someone else*?'

'Yup,' I said weakly. 'That just about covers it.'

Amanda let go of me. She was trembling like a volcano about to blow its top.

But she didn't say another word. She just turned around and walked in through the school gates.

I ran after her.

'I bet there's a perfectly good explanation for it,' I said as she marched up to the front entrance. 'Pippa said they probably arranged the date *weeks* ago, and he couldn't get out of it.' I caught hold of her arm but she shook me off.

'And Mom said *she* went out with a boy called Bobby Mitchell for a little while after she'd met Dad. No, wait, he wasn't called Bobby Mitchell. But it was something like that.' I was scuttling along trying to keep up with Amanda as she went stalking down the corridor with this totally *grim* look on her face.

'Bobby Martin!' I said, remembering. 'His name was Bobby Martin. And Mom went out with him a few times after she'd met Dad because she wanted to let him down easy.

Amanda? See? She didn't want to hurt his feelings. I bet you that's what James was doing with Judy. I just *bet* he didn't want to hurt her feelings.'

'Will you just shut the heck *up*!' Amanda shouted at me. 'You should have told me. You should have told me right away.' She glared ferociously at me. 'I'm never going to trust you again. Stacy! Never!'

She went crashing into the eighth grade locker hallway.

'Has anyone seen that rat James Baker this morning?' she shouted.

Everything went quite. And then people moved back so a gap opened up. And there was James, looking quite shocked.

'What did you call me?' he said.

'A *rat*!' Amanda howled. 'A dirty rotten rat! I just want you to know I hate you, James Baker, and I never want to see you again!'

There was silence for a few seconds. Then someone in the hall said, 'Phew! Way to treat your boyfriend, Amanda!' And a few people laughed.

But James wasn't laughing. He looked like he'd been whacked over the head with a base-ball bat.

Amanda gave a snort and spun on her heel. I guess she'd planned a really dignified exit, except that she'd forgotten I was standing right behind her. She ploughed straight into me.

She knocked me clean off my feet and I landed backside first with a bump on the floor.

Amanda didn't say a single thing. Her expression didn't even change. She just reached down and helped me up and then marched off like nothing had happened.

I heard someone say, 'What did you *do*, James?'

And I heard James say, 'I didn't do *anything*.'

James came over to where I was standing rubbing my backside. He steered me away from the people and around a corner.

'Do you have any idea what that was all about?' he asked.

'She just *found out*!' I said. 'What did you expect her to do? Throw a party?'

'She just found *what* out?'

'People saw you!' I said. '*I* saw you.'

James managed to carry on looking as if he didn't know what I was talking about. Wow, that boy sure can act!

The bell sounded for homeroom.

'I've got to go,' I said. I gave him a hard look. 'You'd better come up with a darned good explanation if you ever want to go out with Amanda again, that's all I can say!' I walked off, but then I thought of an even better final shot. I turned and gave him my fiercest look.

'And if you don't want to go out with Amanda any more, I hope you feel really *good* about yourself for breaking her heart!'

'You're crazy!' James said, shaking his head. 'You're both totally crazy!'

I had to make a stop in the lavatory. I felt all choked up. I guess I was just feeling sorry for Amanda. After all, James had been her first *real* boyfriend, and now it was all over. And I'd have to be on Amanda's side about the break up. Which meant I'd never be able to talk to James again either.

And the problem was that I really liked James, even though I wouldn't be able to forgive him for choosing Judy MacWilliams over Amanda.

Judy MacWilliams. There's a girl I'd like to see smeared all over with honey and thrown in a pit filled with tiger ants! Very *hungry* tiger ants. It was *all* Judy's fault!

Chapter Ten

There was a really big blow-up between James and Amanda outside the cafeteria at lunch time. I *know*. I was caught between them.

I felt sort of *protective* towards Amanda. I mean, when a person loses her first boyfriend to her arch-enemy, she needs all the friends she can get. Which was why I went to Amanda's locker at lunch time so I could be with her and give her some moral support.

'What do *you* want?' she snapped.

'Nothing,' I said.

'Well, you can have that,' Amanda said as she walked off. 'As much as you want!'

I trotted after her.

'Do you want to talk it through?' I asked. 'It always helps to talk about things like this.' I knew that was the right thing to say – it's what psychologists always say on TV when people are suffering from major traumas.

'Get lost, Stacy!' Amanda said.

Psychologists never get *that* response on

TV. But then no psychologist ever had to deal with Amanda.

'Why are you following me?' Amanda asked as we headed to the cafeteria.

'I'm not following you,' I said. 'I just happen to be going the same way as you.' I decided to take her mind off her major trauma. 'Have you thought any more about Cindy's card?'

'No, I haven't thought any more about Cindy's card,' Amanda said. 'I can honestly say I haven't given Cindy's stupid card a single tiny little eensie-weensie thought. In case you hadn't noticed, Stacy, I've got *other* things on my mind right now.'

And, right on cue, the *other thing* that was on Amanda's mind suddenly appeared in front of us. James, that is.

'OK,' James said, staring at Amanda. 'Do you want to explain what all *that* was about this morning?'

'Don't act all innocent with *me*,' Amanda said. 'You know what it was about. It was about *her*!'

She marched straight past James. I tailed along after her. We came to the main corridor that led to the cafeteria and joined the stream of people heading for their lunch.

James caught up with us.

'Her *who*?' he asked.

'Your girlfriend, Judy,' Amanda snarled.

'Judy?' James said. 'What's Judy got to do with anything?'

'Are you going to stand there and tell me you didn't go to the movies with Judy last Saturday?' Amanda hollered, coming to a halt in the middle of the line and glaring at James. 'Stacy saw you!'

'I don't know what Stacy thought she saw,' James said fairly calmly. 'But she *didn't* see me going to the movies with Judy.'

'Are you saying my sister is a liar?' Amanda bellowed. She had everyone's attention by then. Even people who had gone in through the doors of the cafeteria came back out to see what all the noise was about.

I spotted out of the corner of my eye that one of the people who had come back out was Maddie Fischer.

'No, I'm not saying she's lying,' James said, his voice getting louder now as well. 'I'm saying she was wrong.'

'So Judy wasn't there?' Amanda said. 'Or maybe you weren't there? Or perhaps neither of you were there? Perhaps Stacy dreamed the whole thing! Is that what you're saying?'

'I was there,' James shouted. 'I'm not saying I wasn't there. And Judy was there. But we weren't *together*! She was with a bunch of her friends, and I was with a bunch of *my* friends.'

'You were kissing in the back row!' By now I guess Amanda could be heard all over the school.

James looked totally amazed at this.

'Can we talk about this somewhere a little more private?' he said.

'Sure,' Amanda said, and she went zooming off down the corridor. James followed her.

'This is better than TV!' said someone. But now that the entertainment was over, people carried on into the cafeteria.

I went in as well. Maddie Fischer went scuttling over to where Judy MacWilliams was sitting and started babbling to her. I saw a huge great grin spread itself right across Judy's face.

I was really angry with her. I stepped out of the line and marched over to her table.

'Well, I hope you're satisfied!' I said to Judy. 'It looks like your nasty little plan has worked!'

Judy just smiled at me. 'I don't know what you're talking about,' she said. 'You can't blame me if James finally sees the light and realizes what he's missing out on while he was wasting his time with Amanda.'

'Yeah,' Maddie simpered. 'Who'd want to date a bubblehead like Amanda?' And she came out with one of her horrible blubbery giggles.

'Amanda is not a bubblehead,' I said angrily, glaring at Judy. 'And at least Amanda isn't the sort of *feeb* who needs a big *toad* hanging around her to tell her how wonderful she is!'

I decided that was a good insult to leave them with. Cindy and the guys were over at our usual table, so I want straight over to them.

'What's all the excitement?' Pippa asked.

I gave them a quick run-down on what had just happened.

'But you're always saying that Amanda is the dumbest thing on two legs,' Fern said, after I'd told them about my great parting insult to Judy.

'That's different,' I said. 'I'm her sister. I'm allowed to say stuff like that. But I'm not having some total blob like Maddie Fischer going around bad-mouthing her.'

I kept an eye on the cafeteria doors for a while, expecting Amanda to turn up. But she didn't appear and later on when I went looking for her, there was no sign of her anywhere.

I guessed I was going to have to wait to find out what James had said to her.

★ ★ ★

I went to Fern's house after school to play with Lucky for a while, but I didn't get home very late. Mom was upstairs giving Sam a bath. That always involved a whole lot of splashing and chuckling and kicking and giggling. (And that's just *Mom*!)

I offered to help, but Mom said it would be more helpful if I went and cheered Amanda up.

Apparently Amanda had arrived home looking really blue.

'She doesn't want to talk about it,' Mom told me. 'But I'm pretty sure she's had some kind of fight with James.'

I didn't think it was a good idea to tell Mom *everything* right then, but I did fill her in on one detail: me seeing James with Judy.

'Judy MacWilliams?' Mom said. 'Oh, yes, she's that pretty girl with the long black hair, isn't she? The one who caused all that trouble at Amanda's birthday party.' (I don't have time right now to fill you in on that. You'll just have to take my word for it that there was *some* bust-up between Amanda and Judy, and that Judy came off worst.)

'No wonder Amanda is feeling a little down,' Mom said, and then she spluttered as Sam slooshed a whole sloosh of soapy water right up her nose.

Sam gurgled and kicked and laughed and

splashed and there was more bathwater in the air than there was in the tub.

'I'm out of here,' I said. 'Oh, and by the way, Mom, don't let Amanda hear you calling Judy *pretty*. She'll go wild!'

Amanda wasn't in her room. She wasn't in the living room. She wasn't in the kitchen either.

I stood in the middle of the kitchen.

'Ama-a-a-anda!' I called. 'Come out, come out, wherever you are! It's your ever-loving sister here, come to cheer you u-u-up!'

There was a bang on the backdoor. 'Out here,' I heard Amanda's voice.

I found her sitting on the edge of the patio with her face in her fists and her elbows on her knees, looking like the winner of Salesperson of the Year for *Gloom Incorporated*.

I sat next to her. 'Aren't you cold out here?' I asked.

'Nope,' Amanda said, staring out across the lawn.

'Did James say anything much?'

'Nothing that made any sense.' She sighed the deepest sigh I'd ever heard. 'He said it was just a *coincidence* that Judy was there. He said that Judy *was* fooling around, grabbing hold of him and fluttering her eyelashes at him while they were waiting to go in to see the film. He said *that* must have been what

93

you saw. And he said that anyone who said they'd seen him kissing Judy was a total liar, because they didn't sit anywhere near each other.'

'Do you believe him?' I asked cautiously.

'No,' Amanda said miserably.

'So you think he really likes Judy?'

'Don't know. Don't care,' Amanda said. 'And I don't want to talk about it.'

She looked at me. 'You know what he said? He said how could I write him weird letters telling him I was going to love him for always on one day and then bawl him out in front of everyone the next? I *told* him I hadn't written him any letters. And he said, oh, *sure*. And I said, trust me, I didn't write you any letters. And he said, yeah, like you trust me about not kissing Judy. And I said, you *did* kiss Judy. And he said, you *did* write that weird letter. And I said, if you were so innocent, how come you were avoiding me all day yesterday? And he said, because of all the weird stuff you said in that letter. I was afraid you were going to ask me to marry you! And I said, don't worry, I wouldn't marry you if you were the last boy on earth. And he said, that's just fine, 'cos I'd say no. And I said, don't kid yourself, buddy, I wouldn't give you the satisfaction. And he said, I guess we're splitting up, then. And I said, you're darned right we're splitting up. I don't ever want to see you again!' Amanda choked a little and turned her face away. 'And he said, that's fine with me.'

'Are you OK?' I asked.

'Sure. I'm OK,' Amanda said. 'I've got something in my eye, that's all.'

I went into the kitchen and fetched a box of tissues.

Amanda blew her nose and snuffled into the tissue.

'I mean,' she said, rubbing her eyes, 'where does that guy get off, accusing me of writing him a weird letter? He's nuts!'

I looked unhappily at her. Was this a good time to confess?

'Uh, Amanda,' I said. 'I need to tell you something.'

'But why would he make up stuff about some letters?' Amanda said.

'Er, *a* letter, Amanda,' I said. 'Just one letter.'

'Hey, maybe someone *has* written him a letter, pretending it was from me,' Amanda said sharply. 'Some dumb love letter meant to make me look like a total jerk.' She stared at me with red-rimmed eyes. 'I bet that's what happened!' Her eyes went really narrow and evil-looking. 'If I find out who did that, do you know what I'm going to do to them?'

'Uh, no,' I said nervously. 'What are you going to do to them, Amanda?'

'You don't want to *know* what I'm going to do to them, Stacy,' Amanda said. 'You don't want to hear about the things that I'm going to do to them when I find out who they are.' She was making these really alarming ripping and tearing and clawing and gouging movements with her hands while she was speaking.

Then she seemed to calm down a little.

She rubbed her sleeve across her eyes and gave me a really friendly smile. She even put her arm around me and gave me a squeeze.

'You're an OK, sister, Stacy,' she said. 'Thanks for listening to all my blabbing.'

'No problem,' I squeaked as she hugged the breath out of me. All that cheerleading Amanda did had sure put some muscle on her arms.

'What was it you wanted to tell me?' she asked.

'Uh, when?'

'Just now. You said you needed to tell me something. What was it?'

I tried to come up with something.

'Er, we've started collecting photos from people at school for Cindy's card,' I said.

'Oh, Cindy's card,' Amanda said. 'Yeah, I'll have to start thinking about that soon.'

'We're going to the art shop to buy some

paper later in the week,' I said. 'Maybe you could do the front over the weekend?'

'Sure I will, Stacy,' Amanda said. 'No problem.' She stood up and plodded inside. 'After all,' I heard her mumble to herself, 'what *else* will there be for me to do?'

Well, at least now my mind was made up about that letter. I was not, *not*, NOT going to tell her about it.

I just hoped James wouldn't bring it in to school for any reason. Even though I'd written it in block capitals, I had a real suspicion that Amanda would be able to figure out whose writing it was.

And if Amanda found out I'd written that letter, my days as an 'OK sister' would come to a pretty sudden end, that was for sure.

Like they say: ignorance is bliss. And if I had anything to do with it, so far as that letter was concerned, Amanda was going to be one totally blissful big sister.

I hoped.

Chapter Eleven

A word from Professor von Allen, of Pain-in-the-Brain College, Indiana:
So, Stacy, what's the problem? Either Judy and her friends are telling the truth about James going to the movies with Judy and kissing her and all that kind of stuff, or James and his friends are telling the truth and James didn't even sit next to Judy in the movie theatre. All you've got to do is to figure out which one is telling the truth. It's as simple as that!

Yeah, thanks, Prof. It's as simple as *that*, huh? How am I meant to know who is telling the truth? Judy's friends are all saying one thing, and James's friends are saying the exact *opposite*, and I'm here in the middle without the least idea of what really happened!

★ ★ ★

We were on our way to the bus stop the next morning when Amanda suddenly grabbed hold of me.

'I'm so dumb!' she said. 'The *letter*! Of

course! I've *got* it! Remember last night I figured that James wasn't making it up about the stupid love letter?' Amanda said. 'I've just worked out who it must have been! Judy!'

'Why would Judy send James a love letter from *you*?' I asked.

'Think about it,' Amanda said. 'It must have been sent by someone who really dislikes me. Someone who wants me and James to split up, and someone who's smart enough to know that the last thing a guy wants when he's only just started going out with a girl is a letter telling him how much she adores him.'

'Uh, wouldn't a boy be really *pleased* to get a letter like that?' I said. 'I thought that if you'd been going out with a person for a few weeks, you'd really want to know that they liked you a whole lot.'

Amanda patted me on the head. 'You're so cute sometimes, Stacy,' she said. 'You don't know *one* thing about dating, do you?'

'What do you mean?' I asked, trying to ignore being treated like Fido the dog.

'You have to play it cool,' Amanda explained. 'Guys like a challenge. You have to keep them guessing, Stacy. No one in their right mind would confess undying love to a guy after a couple of weeks.'

'Three weeks,' I reminded her.

'Three weeks, six weeks, six *months*,'

Amanda said. 'You still have to keep a guy on his toes. And you don't do that by telling him that you're crazy about him. You've got to make sure he puts a little *effort* into it, Stacy. Besides which, love letters are the pits. Any normal guy would run a mile from a girl who'd send him a *love* letter. And Judy *knows* that!'

One thing I wanted to avoid was Amanda accusing Judy of writing the letter. I could see what would happen then. James would be told to bring the letter in for examination. And despite the capital letters, Amanda might spot that it was my writing. And then I'd be killed.

I sat next to Fern on the bus.

'If you really liked a boy,' I asked her, 'would you tell him or would you keep him guessing?'

'I don't like any boys,' Fern said.

'Yeah, but if you *did*.'

'I don't.'

'Fake it, Fern, for heaven's sake!' I said. 'Help me out, here. Imagine that you really like some boy. Try!'

Fern shut her eyes tight. 'OK,' she said. 'Here goes. I'm trying to imagine liking a boy.' She started pulling these really horrible faces. 'Can't . . . quite . . . get a grip on it,' she said. 'Nope.' She opened her eyes and grinned at me. 'Sorry, Stacy. No can do.'

Yeah, right. Thanks, Fern. Big help.

Brandon De Ville was hanging around by the school gates as we all piled off the bus. He was in his usual leather jacket and sunglasses. He was leaning against the brick gatepost with one leg crossed over the other and a really self-satisfied grin across his face.

What a total dork! Did he really think he looked cool? He looked dumb, that was what he looked. No girl in her right mind could possibly find him attractive.

Amanda nearly trampled me into the ground as she headed over to where Brandon was standing.

'Hi,' she said, clutching her schoolbooks and wriggling like a worm on the end of a fishing line. (Amanda thinks this *wriggling* business makes her look cute. I think it makes her look like she needs to go to the bathroom.)

'Hi,' he said, grinning like an explosion in a tooth factory.

'I'll catch up with you,' I said to Fern. I went over to where Brandon and my stupid sister were standing and gawping at each other.

'Can I talk to you for a minute, Amanda?' I asked.

'Later,' Amanda said, shushing me away with her hand like I was a pesky fly.

'I hear your boyfriend and you had a bust up yesterday,' Brandon said to her.

'It was no big thing,' Amanda said airily. 'I found out he has really bad taste in people.'

Brandon nodded. 'I told you he was a loser.'

'Amanda?' I interrupted. 'I want to *talk* to you.' I had to get her away from that creep. Couldn't she see what a slimeball he was? Was she totally *stupid?*

'I guess you did,' Amanda said, ignoring me. 'Are you always right about things like that?'

'Pretty much,' Brandon said. 'I'm a good judge of character.'

'And have you got any opinions about my character?' Amanda asked in a really sickening, simpery way.

'You're the kind of girl who knows a good thing when she sees it,' Brandon said.

'Uh-huh?'

'Sure. That's why you're coming to the dance with me on Friday.'

'I am?'

'You know you are.'

I couldn't take much more of this. 'Amanda!' I yelled.

She turned on me. 'Stacy! Get *lost*!' she snarled.

'Fine!' I said. 'Just fine, Amanda. I can take a hint.'

I turned and marched off.

That was it! I was through trying to help my sister out. If she wanted to date a *gangster* then that was just fine by me. And if James Baker wanted to date the single most evil girl in the state of Indiana, then he deserved everything that happened to him! If he preferred Judy to Amanda, then he needed to have his head examined.

And I guess I'd have carried *on* feeling that way about it if not for something that I overheard between classes that morning.

It happened like this. We only had a few days to organize Cindy's Bon Voyage card. Which meant we had to start getting the photographs together for sticking inside.

I delegated Pippa and Fern to ask all the guys in our class to bring in photos – and to make it really clear to them that Cindy *mustn't know* about it. And it was my job to ask Ms Fenwick if we could have a photo of her for the card.

I caught up with Ms Fenwick near the teachers' rest room. She seemed really pleased at being asked and she promised to look for a photo and bring it in by the end of the week.

Now, normally, I wouldn't have been in that part of the school at all, so I guess it was *fate* that I happened to see Judy and Maddie

Fischer slinking down a flight of stairs that only led to some basement storerooms.

I kept out of sight until I heard them go through the swing-doors at the bottom of the stairs. Then I crept down after them. I knew darned well they weren't supposed to be down there.

I pushed the door open just a fraction of an inch. There they were, sitting on some old desks in among heaps and piles of discarded school equipment. And I could see right away *why* they'd gone down there.

They were smoking! They lit cigarettes while I watched them through the slit in the door. Maddie took a suck of her cigarette and collapsed into coughing and hawking while clouds of smoke blew out of her mouth.

Judy rolled her eyes.

'You're just never going to be cool, Maddie, until you learn to smoke properly,' she said.

'But it tastes awful,' Maddie coughed.

'That's not the point,' Judy said. 'It *looks* good.' She took a puff on her cigarette. 'If we keep *practising*, (cough!) eventually we'll get to like it, OK? (cough, splutter!) you know what they say: no pain, no gain.'

I noticed Maddie was going kind of green.

'If you say so, Judy,' Maddie groaned. Judy winced as Maddie collapsed into another fit of coughing. Judy wasn't actually smoking her cigarette; she just waved it around while she was speaking.

'Anyway,' Judy said. 'How does it feel to be friends with the smartest girl in town? By the end of this week Amanda is going to feel so *small* she'll have to look up to speak to a *worm*!'

My ears went *zing*! The fact that Judy wanted to get one over on Amanda wasn't any kind of news, but from what she said, it sounded like she had finally come up with a mega-anti-Amanda-plan.

'I don't get it,' Maddie said between bouts of coughing.

'What don't you get, *now*?' Judy sighed.

'Well,' Maddie said, 'didn't you tell me that James Baker was just a prawn?'

'A *pawn*,' Judy said. 'A *pawn*, not a *prawn*. Don't you know what a pawn is?'

'Sure I do,' Maddie said. 'It's one of those small doodas that you play chess with. I'm not *stoopid*, Judy, I'm – *haak, haak, haaaak!*' She doubled up with coughing while Judy whacked her on the back.

'I'm OK, now,' Maddie groaned. 'But what I don't get is why you want to get James to take you to the dance. I didn't think you liked him.'

'It's just part of the big picture,' Judy said. 'The masterplan for the total humiliation of

Amanda Allen.' Judy grinned like a starving crocodile. 'First I split her and James up, with the help of that nerdy pipsqueak sister of hers.'

Nerdy pipsqueak sister? Hey! She's talking about *me*! Grrr! What a total *lizard* that girl is!

'And now,' Judy continued, 'I'm going to sweet-talk James into taking me to the dance.' She gave a nasty little laugh. 'You *know* what I've got planned for Amanda *then*. That's where Brandon comes in.'

Brandon! BRANDON? Brandon De Ville was in on Judy's revenge plan? Now, *that* was something worth knowing.

Right then the warning bell rang for the start of classes.

Judy jumped down off the table and headed for the door I was standing behind.

'Come on,' she said in a really sarcastic voice. 'We don't want to be late for class.'

I went up those stairs like a bullet. Boy, did I have plenty to think about for the rest of the morning!

Chapter Twelve

Judy's Masterplan
(As far as I could figure it out.)
1. Split Amanda and James up, with *my* help. (All the drooling over him at the movies last week was for my benefit. So I'd tell Amanda and she'd get mad and dump him. Except that I *didn't* tell Amanda. But that didn't make any difference, because Judy also got Maddie to go around telling people about the date.)
2. Get James to take *her* to the dance instead of Amanda. (But Maddie said that Judy doesn't even *like* James. Which means she's only going to go to the dance with him to hurt Amanda.)
3. Something involving Brandon De Ville. (I don't know how Brandon fits into the masterplan at all. But I do know he's asked Amanda to go to the dance with him, and I've got a bad feeling she's going to say yes.)

4. Amanda's final humiliation. (How? What? Where? At the dance, maybe? Is this where Brandon comes into it? Are he and Judy going to do something at the dance to totally humiliate Amanda?)

Stacy's Masterplan

1. Tell James about Judy's plan.
2. Tell Amanda about Judy's plan.
3. Get James and Amanda back together again.
4. Accept the undying gratitude of J and A.

Easy, huh? And I was going to put the first step into action as soon as the lunch bell rang. I had to warn James before Judy got to him.

'Stacy, is there something of particular interest going on outside?' Ms Fenwick snapped.

I jumped bolt upright in my desk. I guess I'd been staring out the window while I'd been thinking.

'No,' I said.

'Then would you please pay attention?' Ms Fenwick said. 'I'm not talking for my own amusement.'

I did my best to concentrate, but the Judy, Amanda, James thing kept spinning around in my head and I got in trouble twice more for not listening.

The lunch bell rang and we all headed for the door.

But then: disaster!

'I'd like a word, Stacy,' Ms Fenwick said. Arrgh! She was keeping me behind. Didn't she realize I had to get out of there and find James before Judy sank her fangs into him?

I got a lecture about being attentive in class. Ms Fenwick said she understood that I was *preoccupied* with Cindy's *imminent departure*, but that I shouldn't let it *divert my attention* from my work. As if Cindy was my only worry right then!

I said *yes* and *no* in the right places until she let me go. Cindy and the others were waiting for me in the hall.

'Can't stop!' I said as I flew past them. 'I'll explain later!'

I zipped up the stairs to the cafeteria. I ran along the line, searching for James. He wasn't there. I ran in through the doors. *Still* no sign of him. Then I caught sight of Buddy Hallett, one of James's friends.

'Have you seen James?' I panted. 'It's really important.'

'He's in the gym, I think,' Buddy said. 'What do – '

Vooooom! I was out of there and down the stairs before you could say *pommel horse*.

James is an amazing gymnast and all-round athlete. He spends a lot of his free time training in the gym.

I ran straight into the gym teacher and got my second lecture of the day. This time it was on why I shouldn't go *careering* about the school like some kind of *demented pachyderm*, because I could cause an accident.

'Yes. No. *Yes*. Sorry.'

Don't teachers ever realize that people have *important* things to do? And why do teachers use such weird *words*?

I *walked* into the gym to look for James.

Some girls were playing volleyball, but there was no sign of James. Where could he be?

I stood outside the boys' locker room and called his name through the door. Nothing.

I remembered there was a vending machine down a short flight of stairs at the end of the corridor, and I headed for that.

Sure enough, as I came around the corner, I heard a voice from down the stairs. Heck! Double heck! It was Judy's voice.

'I guess you're looking for someone to go to the dance with,' she was saying. 'Now that you and Amanda have split up.'

I came to a halt. She was with James. They were standing by the vending machine at the side of the stairs. I could see them, but unless they turned and looked up, they wouldn't know I was there.

'Who says we've split up?' James said.

'Oh, come on,' Judy said. 'Everyone knows it after that scene Amanda made outside the cafeteria yesterday.' Judy flicked her hair over her shoulder and gave a snooty little toss of her head. 'Personally, I don't know what you saw in her in the first place. A guy like you could do so much better for himself.'

Ew! Yuck! Talk about *slimey*!

'You think so?' James said.

'Uh-huh,' Judy said. 'Like, for instance *I* don't have a firm date for Friday night. I've had plenty of offers, but I haven't made my mind up yet. If a nice guy was to ask me to the dance, I might just say yes.'

I held my breath.

'Judy, there's something I'd like to ask you,' James said.

'There is?' Judy simpered.

'Why did you go around the school telling people that you and I were going out together?'

I could almost *see* Judy go rigid with surprise.

'I did no such thing,' she said.

'Not personally,' James said. 'You got Maddie to do it for you.' He shook his head.

'You know, that stuff you did at the movies really had me fooled for a while. It wasn't until I found out that Amanda's sister was there that I figured out what you were up to.'

'I don't know what you're talking about,' Judy said.

'I think you do,' James said. 'You wanted to split me and Amanda up. What I don't get is *why*?'

I saw Judy reach out and put her hand on James's arm.

'It's true,' she said. 'I *did* want you to stop going out with Amanda. But only because I wanted to go out with you.' She put her other hand on his arm. 'I know I've been selfish and unkind to Amanda, but it was only because I wanted you to myself. Look, James, I really like you. And however it happened, the thing between you and Amanda is over.'

She moved closer to him. 'You do *like* me just a *little*, don't you, James?'

'I guess so,' James said. (No-o-o-o! James! She doesn't really like you at all! Don't fall for it!) 'I guess I do like you a little.' He pulled away from her and held his hand up in front of her face, his fingers about a tenth of an inch apart. 'About *this* little!' he said. 'And I *dislike* you about *this* much!' He spread his arms wide apart.

'Wha-a-at?' Judy gasped.

'Let me tell you something, Judy,' James said. 'Maybe you have wrecked things between Amanda and me, but I wouldn't go on a date with you if you were the last person in the world.'

Wow! Way to go, James!

'You, you – ' Judy spluttered. 'You total geek!' She put her fists on her hips. 'And to think I was actually going to let people *see* me with you at the dance. Huh! I should have known better than to expect anything from the kind of dork who'd want to date Amanda.'

Judy turned and came stamping up the stairs with a look on her face that would have turned milk sour.

'Get out of my way, freakface!' she snarled at me.

I stepped aside and let her go past.

She crashed through the doors like an out-of-control tank.

James looked up the stairs at me.

'Hi, Stacy. What are you doing here?'

'I was looking for you,' I said. I ran down and sat on the stairs. He sat next to me and I told him the whole story.

'I knew Amanda and Judy didn't get along,' he said. 'But I didn't realize it was *that* bad!'

'It sure is,' I grinned at him. 'But don't you see?' I said. 'All we've got to do now is to tell Amanda all about Judy, and then you guys can get back together again, and everything will be totally brilliant.'

'It's not really as easy as that,' James said. 'I told Amanda that there was nothing going on between me and Judy, but she didn't believe me.' He looked sadly at me. 'I'm not sure if I want to spend time with someone who doesn't trust me, Stacy. And I'm really not sure I can trust her, either. She did something really strange.'

'What did she do?' I asked.

'She wrote me a crazy letter,' James said. 'And there was some really weird stuff in it about wanting to be with me forever.' He spread his hands out. 'I mean, I really like her, but we've only been going out for a few weeks. I don't think I can cope with that kind of *intensity*, you know? And then she denied having written it, which is even *weirder*.' He shook his head. 'I mean, who *else* could have written it?'

'Me,' I said softly.

'It had to be her,' James said. 'But when I . . . uh, excuse me? What did you just say?'

'I wrote it,' I mumbled. I looked across at him and gave a weedy grin. 'It seemed like a good idea at the time.'

'*You* wrote it?'

'Uh-huh. When I saw you and Judy together at the movies, I thought you didn't

114

like Amanda any more. And I thought maybe you didn't realize how much she liked being with you, so I thought I'd write a letter to *tell* you how much she liked being with you.' I looked anxiously at him. 'But I guess I overdid it a little.'

I don't think James needed to have laughed *quite* that much. I mean, it wasn't the funniest thing ever in the entire universe!

'I guess the PS was a little ridiculous,' I said. 'That part about her saying she wanted to be with you forever.'

'It did make her sound a little crazy,' James said.

I looked at him. 'It's not true,' I said. 'And Amanda didn't know anything about it. I made the whole thing up. She's never said anything like that to me.'

'So, she doesn't really like me?'

'Yes! Sure she does, but not *that* much.'

'You mean, she kind of half-likes me?' James said.

'No. She likes you a whole lot,' I said. 'But not – hey! Are you making fun of me?'

'Don't you think you deserve it?' James said with a grin.

'I guess I do,' I said. 'But I had a really good reason for what I did. Pippa Kane told me not to.'

James gave me a puzzled look.

'I'll explain,' I said, getting up. 'I'll explain all about Pippa while we go and look for Amanda.'

James stood up as well. 'We're going to look for Amanda?' he asked.

'Sure,' I said. 'And you guys are going to make up, and you're going to go with her to the dance.'

'I'm not sure,' James said. 'There's still the problem about her not trusting me.'

I looked thoughtfully at him. 'This whole thing was set up by Judy,' I said. 'And if you and Amanda don't get back together, she'll *win*. Is that what you want?'

James looked at me for a few moments.

'Let's find Amanda,' he said.

Yessss!

Stay-see! Stay-see!

You know, there are times when I *amaze* myself with my total and utter brilliance!

Chapter Thirteen

Amanda was in the cafeteria, sitting at a table with the Bimbos.

James and I walked up to them. I was so pleased at the way things had worked out that I had a big grin on my face.

'What's with you, tinselteeth?' Cheryl said.

Amanda gave James a really withering look.

'Could we talk, please, Amanda?' James said.

'Sure,' Amanda said. 'Talk away.'

'In private,' James said.

'If you've got something to say, you can say it right here,' Amanda said. 'These guys are my friends. You know what friends are, don't you, James? People you can rely on. People you can *trust*.'

'Amanda, don't!' I said. 'It's not what you think. It's all Judy's fault.'

'I can believe *that*,' Amanda said. She gave James a really sneery look. 'So, come on, what's the excuse? Was Judy too big and strong for you, huh? Couldn't you fight her off?'

There were giggles from the Bimbos.

'Nothing happened between me and Judy,' James said. 'The whole thing was a set up. Judy planned the whole thing to split us up.'

'Well, good for her,' Amanda said. 'I hope you'll be really happy together.'

'They aren't together!' I said. 'They never were together! Judy *faked* it, Amanda. She faked it to hurt you.'

'She shouldn't have bothered,' Cheryl said. 'Amanda's not hurt at all.'

'Yeah,' Rachel added. 'Amanda's going out with someone else now. She doesn't need *you*.'

'Amanda's going to the dance on Friday with Brandon,' said Natalie. 'Who are you going with, James? With Stacy?'

James looked at Amanda.

'Is that true?' he said.

Amanda hesitated for a moment.

'Tell him, Amanda,' Cheryl urged her.

Amanda looked down at the floor. 'Yes, I'm going to the dance with Brandon,' she said. 'He asked me and I said yes.'

James stood there staring at her for a couple of seconds, then turned and walked away without saying a word.

'You *idiot*!' I hollered at Amanda. 'You total, complete, utter and absolute *idiot*!'

I was *so* mad at her that I could have knocked her head against the wall! That might have beaten some sense into her.

Amanda got up without a word and walked out of the cafeteria, the Bimbos trailing along behind her.

I didn't get to speak to Amanda again until later that night when she finally got home from Cheryl's house. I'd decided that whether she liked it or not, Amanda was going to hear the truth, the whole truth, and nothing but the truth, even if I had to tie her to a *chair* and yell it straight into her ear!

'I'm not interested!' Amanda said as I marched into her room.

'Yes, you *are*!' I said. 'James wasn't at the movies with Judy. I got it wrong. Judy set the whole thing up so that I'd see it and tell you. And then Judy got Maddie Fischer to spread rumours that she and James were going out. But it's not true! She did it to get at you. And that Brandon guy is involved as well. I heard Judy and Maddie talking about it.'

I tried to explain it all to Amanda, but she kept wandering around the room, tidying stuff up and making a big effort not to listen to me.

'OK,' she said at last. 'If James is so darned innocent, how come he avoided me all day on Monday?'

I took a deep breath. This was going to be tricky.

'Because of the letter I put under his door telling him you were crazy about him,' I said.

'You did what?' Amanda screamed.

Amanda came flying at me like some kind of homicidal werewolf-girl. The next thing I knew I was sitting out in the hallway staring at Amanda's slammed bedroom door.

I stood up, rubbing my behind. (One way and another my rear end had been *suffering* recently! This was the second time Amanda had dumped me on it.)

I went over to the door.

'Listen to me!' I said. 'I'm sorry about the letter, OK? I thought I was helping. It was a bad idea! But you've got to listen to me. Brandon only asked you to the dance because it was part of Judy's plan!'

The door flew open and I nearly fell on my nose into her room.

'That is such a lie!' she said. 'Brandon asked me because he *likes* me. And I like him. So there!'

She slammed the door again.

'But he's a creep!' I called through the door.

The door swung open again and this time I really did fall on my face into her room.

'Brandon is not a creep, for your information,' Amanda said as I picked myself up.

'He's fun and cool and really cute. And he's not some goody-two-shoes type who would never even *think* of doing anything exciting or *fun*. And that's why I'm going to the dance with him. And you can tell your pal James that I think he's a boring geek and that dating him was about as thrilling as watching paint dry!' Slam!

'Hey, keep the noise down up there!' Dad called from the living room. 'You're drowning out the TV!'

I went into my room and sat on my bed. Benjamin jumped up into my lap for a late-night petting.

'What are we going to do, Benjamin?' I asked him. 'We can't let Judy win like this. James really likes Amanda, and I *know* Amanda likes James underneath it all.'

'Brrrupp,' Benjamin said, kneading at my legs while I stroked his ears.

'Yeah, I know she said he was a geek. But she didn't mean it. Amanda isn't the sort of person to want to be with a creep like Brandon. Do you know what I think? I think we should find out why Brandon is helping Judy.'

'Mroop,' Benjamin said. 'Broop. Brurrrp.'

'Do you know what?' I said, stroking Benjamin's velvety nose with one finger. 'I'm going to do some investigating tomorrow. I'm going to get to the bottom of this.'

121

Chapter Fourteen

Next morning, I told the guys all about Judy's masterplan, and about *my* plans to dig up the dirt on Brandon before my sister made a complete fool of herself with him.

'How did Judy get her hooks into Brandon so quickly?' asked Cindy. 'He's only been here a few days.'

'Maybe she knew him from before,' Pippa suggested.

'Could be,' I said.

'Or maybe she's invented a mind-ray machine,' Fern said. 'And she's zapped him with it so he'll be her slave for the rest of his life.'

'Yeah, *maybe*,' I said. 'I'm going to need some help keeping track of Brandon. We've got to keep him under . . . uh, *sir*-something.'

'Surveillance,' Pippa said.

'Yeah, that's it,' I said. 'We've got to keep him under surveillance.'

'Why?' Cindy asked.

'Because sooner or later he's bound to meet up with Judy,' I explained. 'And when he does, I want to hear what they say to each other.'

We split into two teams. Fern and Pippa in one, Cindy and me in the other. That way we could take turns hanging around near the Target (Brandon) without him getting suspicious.

Surveillance Report

Before school: No sightings. Possible explanation is that Target arrived late.

Between classes: Target spent time talking with some guys about baseball. Fern checked that Judy wasn't disguised as a boy to try and fool us. She wasn't.

Lunchtime: Target ate lunch in the cafeteria and talked with some guys about baseball. Target went outside and stood around talking with some guys about baseball. Target went to the boys' room. Target got suspicious about Fern and Pippa and told them that if they didn't beat it he'd beat it for them. Pippa and Fern said they didn't want to do surveillance any more. I said that was fine, because they'd blown their cover anyway. Cindy and I kept watch on Target from a distance. He spent the rest of lunch break talking to some guys, although we were too far away to hear what they were talking about. (Cindy said it was probably baseball.) No sign of Judy.

'Maybe he'll meet up with Judy after school,' I said as the final bell rang that afternoon. 'If we follow him *now*, maybe we'll catch them together.'

'Forget it,' Fern said. 'I'm not following him all over town for the rest of the day.'

'Me neither,' Pippa added.

I looked at Cindy.

She sighed. 'OK,' she said. 'But only for a little while, Stacy. If he doesn't meet up with Judy in the first half an hour, I'm going home, OK?'

'He *will*,' I said. 'I've got a *feeling* about it.'

Pippa and Fern headed home. Cindy and I went for a stroll around the school to see if we could find Brandon.

We spotted him hanging out with some guys by the gates. They talked for a few minutes and then broke up and headed off in different directions.

Brandon walked in the direction of the mall. Cindy and I trailed him, keeping plenty of space between us and him so he wouldn't notice us.

'I don't think he's meeting Judy,' Cindy said as we followed Brandon into the mall.

'He is,' I said. 'Trust me.'

'But the school bus doesn't come this way,' Cindy said.

'What's that got to do with it?' I asked.

'I saw Judy and Maddie getting on the bus while we were waiting for Brandon to finish yakking with those other guys,' Cindy said.

'Why didn't you *tell* me?'

'I didn't think.'

'*Cindy*!'

She gave me an apologetic look. 'I guess we should just go home,' she said.

'I guess so,' I said. I took one last look at Brandon. He'd gone into a games arcade. I could see him in there surrounded by all those machines with their flashing screens and explosion noises. He was talking to some other boys.

They weren't boys I'd seen before. I guessed they were people he knew from his old school.

'Wait here for me, Cindy,' I said. 'I just want to listen in on what they've got to say.'

Brandon had his back to the entrance of the arcade, so he didn't see me slide in there. I joined a ring of people watching a zitty-faced skinny guy playing *Urban Raider*.

Brandon and the other guys were standing near enough for me to be able to hear them, especially as his friends were pretty loud. They were a rough bunch and some of them were smoking.

'So what's your new school like?' I heard one of the boys ask Brandon.

'It's a dump,' Brandon said. 'And the teachers are all total dorks. Give me three months and I'll be running the place.'

'I'll give you six weeks before you get expelled,' said another of the boys.

'No way,' Brandon said.

'Brandon doesn't wanna be expelled from his new school,' said the first boy. 'He's got a girlfriend there.'

'Hyuh! Hyuh!' a couple of the boys laughed. It sounded like someone unblocking a sink!

'How'd you make out with her, Brandon?' another of the boys asked.

'Who told you I had a girlfriend?' Brandon said.

'Your cousin told my sister,' said another one of the boys. 'And my sister told me.' He laughed. 'And I told everyone else.'

'Well, you can just go tell them it's not true,' Brandon said. 'My cousin Judy's got a really stupid sense of humour.'

My cousin JUDY???

'So, who's this girl?' one of the boys asked.

'Just some girl called Amanda,' Brandon said. 'Judy hates her. She's kind of cute, but she's really dumb. Judy's going to pay me to help screw her up.'

'So, what's the deal?' asked one of the boys.

'There's some dumb dance at the school on Friday night,' Brandon said. 'Judy wanted me to ask Amanda to go with her. I've got to arrange to pick her up at her house and then not turn up. And that's *it*. I get the money, Judy gets her kicks, and Amanda sits at home all night waiting for a date who isn't going to show.' Brandon laughed again. So did the rest of them.

They all seemed to think that it was really funny. I didn't think it was funny at all. I thought it was nasty and despicable and mean! And I was just about to turn around and tell Brandon exactly what I thought of him, when a better idea occurred to me.

Judy wasn't the only person who could come up with sneaky and cunning plans.

I slid out of the arcade and met up with Cindy. I told her the whole deal, about Judy being Brandon's cousin and how she was going to pay him to stand Amanda up on the night of the school dance.

'But she's not going to get away with it,' I told Cindy. 'I've got a plan!'

'Great,' Cindy said. 'What is it?'

I looked at her. 'I don't know.'

'Huh?'

'I mean I don't know *yet*,' I said. 'My plan is that I'm going to come up with a plan! Right now I've got to get home and eat some choc-choc chip cookies, real fast!'

I think best after eating four or five choc-choc chip cookies. Maybe this time, as I needed to come up with the plan of the century, I'd be needing a few more than usual.

★ ★ ★

I was up in my room later that night when I heard Dad yelling from the kitchen.

'Hey, there was almost a whole pack of cookies in here earlier. Where the heck have they gone?'

'You must have eaten them all,' Mom called from the living room. 'Unless we've got mice.'

I heard Dad come stomping out into the hall.

'Yeah!' he yelled. 'Mice called Stacy and Amanda!'

I brushed the crumbs of the last cookie off my jeans and kept real quiet.

It had taken nine cookies. But it had worked. I had a plan. A cunning plan. A cunning and sneaky plan.

The only problem was, I felt a little sick from eating too many cookies.

★ ★ ★

Now, if a person had a *normal* sister, a person could go up to that normal sister and point out to her that she was being taken for a *ride* by a certain new boy at school, and that she would end up being made to look a total fool.

The problem was that I had *Amanda*. Once Amanda got an idea into her head, a person needed some kind of nuclear device to shift it. And the idea that Amanda had in her head was that Brandon had asked her to the dance because he really liked her.

So, the chances were pretty near zero that Amanda would sit still long enough for me to explain that Brandon *didn't* really like her at all, and that it was all part of Judy's evil little plan.

And even if I *did* manage to hammer that idea into her head, she probably wouldn't even believe me. She already knew I liked James. And I hadn't exactly made a secret of the fact I thought Brandon was a creep from the first time I'd seen him.

And it was pretty clear from what had happened in the cafeteria yesterday at lunch that Amanda was being egged on by the Bimbos to go to the dance with Brandon.

In other words, my brilliant plan had to work without Amanda's help. In fact, I'd decided after cookie number nine, it would really only work if Amanda didn't *know* about it.

* * *

Part one of my plan depended on James.

I managed to track him down between classes the next day. We found a quiet corner where we could talk. I told him about Brandon being Judy's cousin and all that. And then I explained that I had a plan. At first he wasn't too keen to listen to me.

'Look, Stacy,' he said, 'you heard Amanda yesterday. She's going to the dance with Brandon.'

'But I just *told* you,' I said. 'Brandon's going to stand her up.'

'But she doesn't know that,' James said. 'As far as Amanda's concerned, she had the choice to go to the dance with me or to go with Brandon.' He shrugged. 'And she chose him.'

'OK,' I said. 'I admit it might *look* like that to someone who doesn't really know my sister. But I know she likes you best. She might not *think* she does right this minute, but that's just because she's kind of . . . *confused*.'

'She is?'

'Sure she is,' I said, nodding. 'Amanda confuses easily. Especially when she's got Bimbos like Cheryl Ruddick and Natalie Smith giving her stupid ideas.'

'She didn't sound confused,' James said.

'She sounded like she didn't want anything to do with me.'

I frowned at him. I could see he was going to need what my mom calls *a good talking-to*.

'Look,' I said. 'Do you like Amanda?'

'Sure, I like her,' James said.

'And do you want to keep going out with her?'

'It's not that simple.'

'Yes or no?'

'Yes.'

'Fine,' I said, 'so, do you want to hear my plan?'

'Shoot,' James said. 'What have I got to lose? Except maybe my *mind*. What's the plan?'

'First,' I told him, 'you've got to arrange to go to the dance with Judy.'

'Hold on,' James said. 'Remember, I told Judy I wouldn't go to the dance with her if she was the last person on earth.'

'So, tell her you changed your mind,' I said. 'Make something up. Tell her you've had time to think it over, and you've decided that you were wrong about her. Tell her you finally realized that she's the most gorgeous and wonderful girl in town.'

'She's not going to fall for that,' James said.

'Sure, she will,' I said. 'She already thinks it herself!'

'OK,' James said. 'I'll give it a try. But then what?'

'You arrange to meet her outside the dance at, say, half past seven,' I told him. 'And then what you do is *this*.'

A grin spread across James's face as I explained my plan to him.

He looked at me when I'd finished.

'You're kind of sneaky for someone your age,' he said. 'I hope this plan of yours works!'

'It will if you can get Judy to agree to go to the dance with you,' I said. 'Why don't you go and look for her now?'

'OK,' James said. 'I'll let you know how things go.'

All I had to do then was to keep my fingers crossed until James got back to me.

Have you ever tried writing with your fingers crossed? In the end Ms Fenwick got so mad at me for dropping my pen all the time that I gave up and sat with my legs crossed instead.

Between classes I kept my fingers crossed. Through classes I kept my legs crossed. And when I couldn't cross either my fingers or my legs, I crossed my eyes.

Chapter Fifteen

'Could I ask you a personal question?' Cindy said as we stood chatting together before lunch the next day.

'Sure,' I said.

'Is there something wrong with your eyes? You keep going like *this*.' She focused her eyes on the end of her nose.

'I'm doing it for luck,' I explained.

'Oh, I see,' Cindy said. 'That's OK, then.'

We continued chatting. It was my job to keep Cindy occupied while Pippa and Fern went around to all the other people in our class gathering photographs for the Bon Voyage card. We had quite a few already, in an envelope in my locker. That evening Fern and Pippa were coming to my house and we were going to start cutting and pasting.

Cindy was telling me about her mom taking a car-load of old toys to the children's ward of the hospital.

'I never realized how much junk there was lying around in our house,' Cindy said. 'I mean, when you're moving all the way across the country, there's plenty of stuff you realize you don't really want any more. Stacy, are you listening to me?'

'Sure, I am,' I said. But something had caught my eye. Way over on the far side of the playground I could see James and Judy walking along together.

It wasn't until I was standing in line for lunch in the cafeteria that I finally found out for certain that my plan was off to a flying start. James walked past me.

'She went for it,' he whispered as he went past.

Judy had agreed to go to the dance with him!

I was dying to ask him all the details, but I didn't think it was a good idea for the two of us to be seen talking to each other. Word might get back to Judy. And Judy wasn't dumb. She might put two and two together and come up with the kind of *four* that would ruin everything.

So, the Judy and James part of my plan was OK. All I had to worry about now was Amanda. Would she behave the way I hoped she would? Or would she do something totally off the wall and mess everything up?

Keep those fingers crossed, Stacy!

*   *   *

Pippa and Fern and I bought a big sheet of white card from the art shop in the mall that afternoon and headed to my house with it. We were going to make Cindy's card out of it.

The hard part had been getting rid of Cindy so we could go buy it in secret. We had to pretend we were all going straight home. I said I'd promised to help my mom. Pippa said her mom was taking her to a concert.

And Fern? Fern said her house had gotten infested with cockroaches and her dad had bought a whole truckload of anti-cockroach spray, and that her and her mom and dad were going to be spending the rest of the day killing cockroaches.

'You're welcome to come along and help,' she'd said to Cindy with a big smile.

'No, thanks,' Cindy had said. 'I think I'll just head home and help my mom clear out the attic.'

The sheet of card was fourteen inches by twenty inches. We cleared my desk and carefully folded the card in half. I used the edge of a pair of scissors to make a neat fold, like Amanda had said. Even folded in half, it was going to be a big card.

Mom lent me a pair of special scissors called *crimping shears*. They're used in dressmaking, and they're made so they cut zig-zag lines.

Fern and Pippa cut the heap of photos into interesting shapes with the shears. I carefully wrote out on the card the special goodbye poem that Mom and I had thought up, using a ruler to make sure the lines were all straight.

Then all three of us pasted the spikey-edged photos on both sides of the inside of the card, leaving enough space for people to write their farewell messages.

We only had one minor disagreement between us when the end of Pippa's braid got dipped accidentally in the paste. Fern said it'd make a perfect paste brush if we cut it off and fixed it onto a handle. Which was all pretty harmless until Fern started waving the scissors around and Pippa went and locked herself in the bathroom and wouldn't come out until Fern promised that she'd only been kidding.

I asked Amanda to come and check the card out and she said it looked just fine. Then Mom came to look and said it was going to be the best Bon Voyage card anyone had ever been given. And then Dad came up and said he almost wished he was leaving town just so someone would give him a card like it.

So, I guess you could say that Dad's idea about the photos, along with Mom's crimping shears and our cutting and pasting had been a big success.

We handed the card over to Amanda and she promised to have the front finished in plenty of time for us to sneak it into school and get everyone to sign it.

Mom drove Pippa and Fern home and then I got ready for bed. The strange thing was that I'd gotten so interested in making the card that I'd kind of forgotten *why* we were making it. Cindy was going away! I still couldn't really believe it.

I couldn't imagine what life would be like without Cindy.

$\star$ $\star$ $\star$

It was late Friday afternoon and I was in the living room playing *whooops!* with Sam. Sam liked a good game of *whoops!*

The rules of whoops!

Sit right on the edge of the couch with your baby brother balanced on your knees and facing you. (Keep a good grip on your baby brother at all times during the game.) Jog your knees up and down so your baby brother is bounced around squealing and giggling. Keeping a good hold of his hands, straighten your legs so he slides down to your feet. While he's sliding say *whoops!*

Lift your baby brother up onto your knees and start all over again.

Play the game over and over until your arms feel like they're falling off. Your baby brother will never get bored with it.

I could hear Amanda charging around upstairs, getting herself ready for the dance. I'd heard her tell Mom that Brandon had arranged to pick her up here at seven o'clock. Mom had agreed to drive the two of them to school.

I was really surprised that Mom hadn't said anything when Amanda had told her that she was going to the dance with a different boy. I'd have expected Mom to ask about James, but she didn't say a single *word*.

Amanda was ready by six o'clock. Of course, the rest of the house was a total wreck by then. That always happened when Amanda went anywhere special. It would be like we had our own pet tornado. Or a hurricane, maybe. Hurricane Amanda.

'Do you want to play with Sam?' I asked Amanda. She was standing behind me, tapping her fingers impatiently on the back of the couch. She was looking at her watch every twelve seconds and groaning about it being so *early*. 'Playing with Sam will make the time pass quicker,' I told her.

'I'm ready to go *out*, in case you've forgotten,' Amanda said. 'I'm sure Brandon will be totally impressed if I open the door to him and I'm covered all over in baby spit.'

I looked round at her. She did look pretty good. She *ought* to; she'd been in the bathroom for an hour and a half!

'What would you do if he didn't show?' I asked.

Amanda stared at me. 'Are you nuts?' she said. 'He was *begging* me to go to the dance with him. There's no way he won't show.'

'What if he was only pretending?' I asked.

'Let me tell you something, Stacy,' Amanda said with her big-know-it-all-older-sister smirk. 'The things you know about *boys* could be written on the head of a needle.'

'You mean a *pin*,' I said. 'Needles don't have heads.'

'No, and neither do *you*,' Amanda said.

I felt like I should tell her the truth. In fact, I probably *would* have if not for that crack about me knowing nothing about boys. Amanda is just so *smug* sometimes that she kind of *asks* to be taken down a peg or two.

Mom came in to take Sam off for his before-bedtime bath.

'Do I look OK?' Amanda asked her.

Mom looked her up and down. 'You look

lovely, sweetheart,' Mom said. 'Except for that smudge on your nose.'

'Whaaat?' Amanda went haring upstairs.

Mom picked Sam up, chuckling to herself. 'She always falls for that!' she said to me. 'Every time!'

There wasn't any smudge on Amanda's nose at all. Sometimes I think I must have inherited my sense of humour from my mom.

I sat and watched TV for a while. Amanda came and kind of hovered, checking her watch and going over to the window and back to see if anyone was coming, even though it was only six thirty.

'Why don't you sit down?' I asked.

'I'll wrinkle my dress.'

'So take it off,' I said. 'You've got half an hour before he's supposed to get here.'

'Oh, right,' Amanda said. 'So, he turns up early and I'm sitting here in my underwear. Great idea, Stacy.'

'Trust me,' I said. 'He won't be early. You can bet on that.'

Amanda frowned at me. 'You just never give up, do you?' she said. 'For some reason, you took a dislike to Brandon from the first time you saw him. Can't you just get it into your thick head that you don't *know* him at all?'

'I know more about him than you do,' I said.

'OK,' Amanda said. 'Come on. Spill the beans. What's the gossip on him in the sixth grade? Was he expelled from his other school for murdering a teacher? Or did he steal the school trophies?'

'I know Judy paid him to ask you to the dance,' I yelled. 'And I know he's not going to show up tonight!'

Amanda just laughed at me.

I got up and walked out. There are times when walking away from an argument is the best thing a person can do. I'd known all along my sister wasn't going to believe a word I said.

'I'm going upstairs,' I said to her as I left the room. 'Maybe you'll feel like listening to me when he doesn't turn up!'

I sat on my bed and waited. That stupid-looking stuffed rabbit sat and grinned at me from across the room until I couldn't stand it any more. I went over and tied his ears together across his face.

I looked at my bedside clock. The minute hand was just coming up to the hour. Seven o'clock.

★ ★ ★

I heard Amanda in the hall.

'Mom, he's *late*. What should I do?'

I heard Mom's voice, but I couldn't hear what she said.

141

It was ten past seven. In twenty minutes, step two of my plan was due to take off.

I heard Amanda stamping up and down the hall. I heard her open the front door and go out. A couple of minutes later I heard her come stomping back in and slam the door.

'There's no sign of him!'

I went out and stood at the top of the stairs. Amanda was sitting on the stairs with her chin in her fists.

'Excuse me,' I said. 'Are you ready to listen to me yet?'

Amanda turned and glared up at me.

'He'll be here,' she snapped.

'He won't,' I said. I sat crosslegged at the top of the stairs. 'He's Judy's cousin, Amanda.'

'Don't be stupid!'

'He won't turn up because Judy *paid* him to ask you to the dance,' I said. 'And part of the deal was that he would stand you up.' I'd expected to enjoy telling Amanda all this, but somehow it didn't quite happen like that. To be honest, I felt really bad about it.

Amanda just looked at me. I couldn't figure out what she was thinking.

'How do you know?' she asked.

I told her the whole story about the Judy/ Brandon plot, right from the beginning. (I didn't tell her about *my* plan. She'd find out about that soon enough.)

She didn't say a word until I finished.

'Why didn't you tell me before now?' she asked in a really quiet voice.

'I tried to tell you about Judy and James,' I said. 'You wouldn't listen.'

Amanda was quiet for a couple of minutes.

'OK!' she said determinedly. 'We'll see about Brandon De Ville!' She pulled her address book out of her bag and flipped it open.

'What are you going to do?' I asked.

'You'll find out,' she said. She stood up and grabbed the phone off the wall. She punched out a number and held the receiver to her ear.

'Oh, hi,' she said into the phone. 'Is Brandon there, please? Yeah? Great? Can I have a word with him, please?' Me? Oh, uh, I'm a friend of Judy's. Yeah, that's right. Thanks.'

She leaned against the wall, examining her nails while she waited for Brandon to come to the phone. Amanda super-cool!

'Oh, hi, Brandon. It's Amanda. Yeah, you *remember*, your *date* for tonight?'

There was a pause. Amanda cradled the phone on her shoulder and took a mirror out of her bag. She tweaked her hair around a little, going 'uh-huh?' every now and then. I could just about hear Brandon's voice. I guessed he was giving her some excuse for why he hadn't showed up.

'Oh, right,' Amanda said in a really sympathetic voice. 'Gee, I'm really sorry about that. Brandon. A twisted ankle, huh? That must be really painful. I'll tell you what.' Suddenly Amanda's voice wasn't so sympathetic any more. 'Why don't I come over to your house and twist your ankle back into shape for you?' She suddenly yelled full-volume into the phone. 'And while I'm there, I can kick you to *death*!'

Wow! That must have rattled his brain!

There was a feeble whine down the phone.

'No, Brandon,' Amanda said in a really hard voice. 'I'll tell *you* what's going to happen, OK? First, you're going to make a miraculous recovery. Then you're going to put on your best clothes and you're going to wash your face and comb your hair. Then you're going to head for the school and wait outside for me. And I'm going to get my mom to drive me over there, and we're going to walk into the dance together. Have you got all that, Brandon? Or do you want me to come over to your house right *now* and explain it all again?'

Oops! That wasn't what I'd expected. All of a sudden my plan wasn't looking quite so healthy any more.

'Good!' Amanda said into the phone. 'I'm glad we got that sorted out, Brandon. I'll see you in about twenty minutes, OK?'

She slammed the phone down.

'I'll teach that lowlife not to mess with *me*,' she said. 'Who does he think he is?!'

'Uh, Amanda,' I said, 'you weren't supposed to do that.'

She looked up the stairs at me.

'So, what was I *supposed* to do? Lock myself in my room and cry myself into a pool of tears? That creep asked me out on a date, and he's darned well going to *take* me out on a date if I have to drag him there by his hair!'

'Listen to me, Amanda,' I said. 'I'd made other plans.'

She frowned. 'Other plans? What other plans? What are you talking about?'

'It was meant to be a surprise,' I said.

Before Amanda had time to say anything the front doorbell rang.

I had a pretty good idea who was on the other side of the door. It was my *other plan*, right on time.

Amanda stalked over to the door.

'What kind of surprise?' she asked, looking at me over her shoulder as she opened the door.

'Hi, Amanda,' James said. He held out a bunch of flowers. 'I bought these for you.'

'*That* kind of surprise,' I said.

Chapter Sixteen

Amanda stared at James. Then she stared at the bunch of flowers.

'I'm sorry,' she said, 'but aren't you at the wrong address? This is the Allen house. Judy lives over in Wood Hill.'

'I know,' James said.

'Hi, James,' I called, running down the stairs.

'Hi, Stacy.'

Amanda took a long look at me over her shoulder, then another long look at James. Then she grabbed the flowers out of his hand and said, 'Wait just a minute, James,' and shut the door on him.

She stalked up to me and put her arm around my shoulders.

'See these?' she said, waving the flowers in my face.

'Uh-huh.'

'Unless you explain exactly what's going on here, I'm going to cram these up your nose.' She gave me a very alarming smile. 'I heard that James had asked Judy to go to the dance. But James is standing on my doorstep. Explain!'

'I got James to ask Judy,' I said quickly as the flowers danced around under my nose. 'And then I told him to be *here* at – ' I took a quick look at my watch, ' – *this* time, because I knew by now you'd have figured Brandon wasn't going to show. I was going to tell you the whole story then. I thought you'd be really upset, see? And then, just when you thought you didn't have a date for tonight, James would arrive, and you and James would go to the dance together and get back together again and . . .' I spread my arms. 'Everything!'

'What about Judy?'

'Well,' I said, 'if *that* went according to plan, she'll be hanging around outside the school waiting for James.' I grinned at Amanda. 'You'll be able to say *hi* as you go in past her with him. Pretty neat, huh?'

'You set all this up without telling me?' Amanda said.

'Uh-huh.'

'To get James and me back together again?'

'Yeah.'

'So, you've been sneaking around behind my back for the past few days, interfering in my life and plotting with James like some kind of total control freak?'

'Uh, well, if you put it like that, yes. I guess so.'

Amanda stared at me and I had the feeling that the flowers were about to disappear up my nose.

Then she smiled.

'You're something else, Stacy,' she said.

I grinned. 'Am I?'

'You'd better believe it.' She let go of me. 'Mom!' she hollered. 'We're ready to go!'

Mom came down the stairs, carrying a very sleepy Sam.

'Can I come along for the ride?' I asked. 'I can keep an eye on Sam.'

'Sure thing,' Mom said. She carefully off-loaded Sam into my arms. 'There you go; you can start right now.'

Amanda opened the door while Mom fetched her car keys.

James was still standing there on the porch, looking kind of like a forgotten parcel.

'Well?' Amanda asked him. 'What are you waiting for? Are we going to this dance or not?'

A huge smile stretched across his face.

'You bet,' he said. 'You look great, Amanda.'

'Thanks,' Amanda said. 'You don't look so bad yourself.' She stepped out and linked arms with him.

'Hi, Mrs Allen,' James said as Mom and I and Sam followed him and Amanda out to the driveway.

'Hi, James,' Mom said, without batting an eyelid about the fact that it was James and not Brandon who had come for Amanda.

We all piled into the car and Mom set off for school. I sat up front with Sam dozing off in my lap. I took a sneaky look at James and Amanda in the mirror. They were sitting close together. Good sign! Then they looked at each other and smiled. Very good sign! Then they both started laughing although no one had said anything funny.

I hoped that was a good sign as well, but you can't always tell with teenagers. They do some pretty weird things.

It wasn't long before Mom steered the car in through the school gates and headed around to the gym, where the dance was being held.

Other cars were coming and going, and other eighth-graders were making their way up the steps and in through the open doors. From out in the parking lot I could see flashing coloured lights through the doorway. And when Amanda opened the car door, I could even hear the dance music playing.

And guess who was standing at the bottom of the stairs in her best party outfit? Standing there with her long black hair shining and her midriff showing and her legs looking about three yards long under the smallest skirt in the state?

Judy had her arms folded, and even from that distance I could see the sour-lemon expression on her face.

'I'll pick you guys up at eleven,' Mom called as James and Amanda headed for the gym.

'Mom, could you hold Sam for just a minute?' I said. 'There's something I don't want to miss.'

I trailed along behind Amanda and James.

Judy was staring at them with her eyes like dinner plates.

'Hi, Judy,' Amanda said. 'Waiting for someone?'

Judy made this strange hissing kind of noise, as if steam was coming out of her ears.

'I'm sorry,' James said to her, 'I'm really sorry I've had to let you down like this, but I found out I had a date after all.'

'Don't sweat it, Judy,' Amanda said. 'Your cousin Brandon should be here any minute.' Gri-i-i-in!! 'I'm sure he'll be really pleased to go to the dance with you. He wasn't able to get a date either.'

Oh, boy! The expression on Judy's *face*!

Amanda and James walked up the steps arm in arm and went into the gym. And if looks could kill, neither of them would have made it past the doorway.

That was all I wanted to see. I ran back to the car. As we drove out, I saw Brandon coming along the sidewalk towards the school entrance. I wouldn't have minded hearing what Judy and Brandon had to say to each other when they met!

'Mom,' I said, 'you did know Amanda and James split up?'

'Yup,' Mom said.

'And you knew Amanda was supposed to go to the dance with a different guy?'

'Yup.'

'Don't you want to know what happened?'

'Nope.'

We drove along in silence while I tried to figure my mom out.

'Amanda and James are back together,' I said.

'That's what I figured,' Mom said. She glanced at me. 'I'll give you a word of advice, Stacy, honey. Don't get involved in your sister's love life. That kind of thing is a regular minefield.'

Wow! If she *knew*! If she only knew!

★ ★ ★

Amanda came gallumphing into my room and crashed down on my bed.

'Stacy? Are you awake?' she said, shaking me like a rag doll.

'I am now!' I gasped. 'What the heck's going on?'

'I just got back,' Amanda said. 'I've got to tell you – it was the most incredible night of my entire life!'

I rubbed my eyes and sat up. Amanda was grinning like a piano keyboard.

'I'm totally worn out!' she said. 'My legs are worn down to the *knees*! We danced all night. James is such a great guy.' She gave a shiver of excitement. Her eyes were shining like searchlights. 'I'm too excited to sleep. I'm going to tell you every single *detail*!'

And she did. I couldn't have ended up knowing more about that dance if I'd been there in person with a camcorder!

In the end Dad had to just about *drag* Amanda out of my room to get her to go to bed. Even then I could hear her telling *him* the whole story again as he marched her off to the bathroom.

Dad came back to my room.

'Goodnight, sweetie,' he said, leaning in through the door. 'Sleep tight!' He closed the door and I was back in darkness again.

Success! Amanda and James were together again! I flopped back in bed.

I just hoped one thing. I hoped Amanda

and James would *stay* together this time. No way could I go through all *that* again!

★ ★ ★

On Cindy's last day at school, we gave her the card and a going-away present. The present was a heart-shaped jewellery box from everyone in class. Cindy didn't have much in the way of jewellery so I bought her a cat brooch to put in the box. Pippa bought her some really nice stud earrings.

Fern brought in a special card from Lucky, with his paw print in it and a photo of him rolling on the floor and looking really dumb and funny and cute and lovable. (Fern's sweater was covered in black paw-prints, too. I guess putting a puppy's paw in an inkpad is easy enough, but getting the puppy to keep his inky paw to himself afterwards is something else!)

Amanda had done a brilliant job on the front cover. She'd included *everything* I'd asked for, up to and including a coloured drawing of Cindy in an aeroplane and cartoons of me and Pippa and Fern waving her goodbye. Cindy got a little choked up when she opened the card and saw all the photos and the messages and the special poem.

I felt a little sniffly after that, too, so I went to the girls' room. I was just finishing my sniffle when Pippa came in and we both started sniffling again. And then Cindy turned up in there and all three of us sniffled together and swapped tissues and promised to write and call and visit and send photos.

Then Fern arrived and asked what all the blubbing was about – the way she *would*!

And Fern said, 'She's only going to California, guys. It's not like she's been abducted by –'

And we all yelled, 'Aliens!' and burst out laughing.

The four of us went for hamburgers that night, and we managed to have a really good time, even though it was such a sad occasion.

In the morning we all went over to Cindy's house. All their furniture was in the moving van. The house looked weird with nothing in it. It looked really *small*. You'd think a house would look bigger without loads of things cluttering it up. But it didn't. It looked *tiny*.

We made double-certain-sure that we had Cindy's new address written down correctly.

Then the Spiegels all got into their car and we waved and waved like crazy as they followed the moving van along the road and around the corner and out of sight.

'Oh, well,' Pippa sighed. 'I guess that's it.' She looked at us. 'Do you guys want to do anything?'

'I promised I'd help Mom in the store,' Fern said. (Her folks run a general store.)

'I think I'll just go home,' I said.

'OK,' Pippa said. 'See you later, huh?'

I cycled slowly home. I felt like I was in some kind of strange dream. Like the whole thing about Cindy leaving wasn't *real*.

I looked at the phone in the hall. And do you know what I almost did? I almost dialled Cindy's old number. Isn't that silly? I mean, I knew perfectly well the line had been disconnected. I guess I just hoped that Cindy would pick up the phone and say, 'Hi, Stacy,' the way she always did. And I'd say, 'Hi, Cindy, are you coming over?' And she'd say, 'Sure, I'll be there in ten minutes.'

I went up to my room. I sat on the floor with my back to Donovan the giant stuffed rabbit and held the smiling pig-stone from San Diego in both hands.

I'm not sure how long I sat there, but it felt like a couple of million years.

There was a thunder of feet up the stairs.

Amanda burst into my room.

'C'mon,' she said, hauling me up off the floor. 'James and I are having lunch at Casey's and then we're going ice skating, and you're coming with us. We're celebrating!'

'Celebrating what?' I asked as I was towed across the landing.

'I don't know,' Amanda said. 'Nothing in particular.'

'I can't skate!' I said as I was dragged down the stairs.

'We'll help you.'

'Mom, help!' I yelled. 'I'm being kidnapped!'

Mom came out of the living room. She was grinning.

'Good,' she said. 'Have a nice time.'

James was waiting for us at the end of the driveway.

And do you know what? After a couple of hours of skating lessons from Amanda and James that afternoon I *still* fell on my behind every five minutes.

It looked like I was going to have to write my first letter to Cindy standing up!

Other great reads from **Red Fox**

Further Red Fox titles that you might enjoy reading are listed on the following pages. They are available in bookshops or they can be ordered directly from us.

If you would like to order books, please send this form and the money due to:

ARROW BOOKS, BOOKSERVICE BY POST, PO BOX 29, DOUGLAS, ISLE OF MAN, BRITISH ISLES. Please enclose a cheque or postal order made out to Arrow Books Ltd for the amount due, plus 75p per book for postage and packing to a maximum of £7.50, both for orders within the UK. For customers outside the UK, please allow £1.00 per book.

NAME_____

ADDRESS_____

_____

Please print clearly.

Whilst every effort is made to keep prices low, it is sometimes necessary to increase cover prices at short notice. If you are ordering books by post, to save delay it is advisable to phone to confirm the correct price. The number to ring is THE SALES DEPARTMENT 0171 (if outside London) 973 9000.

Other great reads from **Red Fox**

Little Sister Series by Allan Frewin Jones

LITTLE SISTER 1 – THE GREAT SISTER WAR

Meet Stacy Allen, a ten year old tomboy and a bit of a bookworm. Now meet her blue-eyed blonde sister, Amanda, just turned 13 and a fully-fledged teenager. Stacy thinks Amanda's a total airhead and Amanda calls Stacy and her gang the nerds; they have the biggest love-hate relationship of the century and that can only mean one thing – war.
ISBN 0 09 938381 0   £2.99

LITTLE SISTER 2 – MY SISTER, MY SLAVE

When Amanda starts to become a school slacker, Mom is ready to take drastic action – pull Amanda out of the cheerleading squad! So the sisters make a deal; Stacy will help Amanda with her school work in return for two whole days of slavery. But Amanda doesn't realize that when her little sister's boss, two days means 48 *whole* hours of chores – snea-kee!
ISBN 0 09 938391 8   £2.99

LITTLE SISTER 3 – STACY THE MATCHMAKER

Amanda is mad that the school Barbie doll, Judy McWilliams, has got herself a boyfriend, and to make things worse it's hunky Greg Masterson, the guy Amanda has fancied for ages. Stacy feels that it's her duty as sister to fix Amanda's lovelife and decides to play cupid and do a bit of matchmaking, with disastrous results!
ISBN 0 09 938401 9   £2.99

LITTLE SISTER 4 – COPYCAT

Cousin Laine is so coo-ol! She's a glamorous 18 year old and wears gorgeous clothes, and has got a boyfriend with a car. When Stacy and Amanda's parents go away for a week leaving Laine in charge, 13 year old Amanda decides she wants to be just like her cousin and begins to copy Laine's every move . . .
ISBN 0 09 938411 6   £2.99

Other great reads *from* **Red Fox**

Little Sister Series by Allan Frewin Jones

LITTLE SISTER 5 – SNEAKING OUT

Pop star Eddie Eden is *the* guy every cool teenager is
swooning over and Amanda has got a mega crush on him.
Amanda is in love big time and when Eddie's tour dates are
announced she's desperate to see her idol – but Mom and
Dad don't want her out so late. So what else is there for a
love-struck girl to do but sneak out?
ISBN 0 09 938421 3   £2.99

LITTLE SISTER 6 – SISTER SWITCH

Stacy's pen pal, Craig, loves her letters and all his friends are
jealous when they see her photo – so he fixes a date. This is
bad news for the Allen sisters. Stacy hates her mousy hair
and freckles so much that she sent him a photo of pretty
Amanda. But if Stacy can persuade Amanda to swop places
and be *her* for one day she might be able to keep her secret
identity safe . . .
ISBN 0 09 938431 0   £2.99

BESTSELLING FICTION FROM RED FOX

☐ Blood	Alan Durant	£3.50
☐ Tina Come Home	Paul Geraghty	£3.50
☐ Del-Del	Victor Kelleher	£3.50
☐ Paul Loves Amy Loves Christo	Josephine Poole	£3.50
☐ If It Weren't for Sebastian	Jean Ure	£3.50
☐ You'll Never Guess the End	Barbara Wersba	£3.50
☐ The Pigman	Paul Zindel	£3.50

PRICES AND OTHER DETAILS ARE LIABLE TO CHANGE

ARROW BOOKS, BOOKSERVICE BY POST, PO BOX 29, DOUGLAS, ISLE OF MAN, BRITISH ISLES

NAME...

ADDRESS...

....

....

Please enclose a cheque or postal order made out to B.S.B.P. Ltd. for the amount due and allow the following for postage and packing:

U.K. CUSTOMERS: Please allow 75p per book to a maximum of £7.50

B.F.P.O. & EIRE: Please allow 75p per book to a maximum of £7.50

OVERSEAS CUSTOMERS: Please allow £1.00 per book.

While every effort is made to keep prices low it is sometimes necessary to increase cover prices at short notice. Arrow Books reserve the right to show new retail prices on covers which may differ from those previously advertised in the text or elsewhere.